NAHANNI

David M. Mannes

ISBN: 978-1-894936-81-1
Copyright © 2007 David M. Mannes
All Rights Reserved
Saga books
Sagabooks.net
Cover Photography Kim Wolff

DISCLAIMER:
Although based on reported events, Nahanni is a work of fiction.
Historic personages appear in the novel but some literary license has
been taken. All characters are fictitious and any similarity to a real
person living or dead is purely coincidental.

Acknowledgements

A novel's path to publishing is a long one and there are a number of people who must be thanked to help make this dream possible. Thanks to Ruth Thompson and the editors and staff at Saga Books, for seeing the potential of this book and agreeing to publish it.

I'd also like to thank Carl Stewart and Marsha Woods who read earlier versions of this novel and whose enthusiasm, comments and criticisms helped me refine this effort.

Thanks to Kim Wolff whose fortuitous canoe trip through the Nahanni area, and his prodigious photography provided me with cover photographs.

Thanks to my daughter Samantha for helping to design the cover.

To the rest of my family fan club: my wife Sandy, and my son Josh ☺

"Of all the deaths recorded here, overlooking Weir's and O'Brien's which police did not investigate; there is one aspect common to all which appears to have been overlooked by myth-makers. Take a quick look over the account of each of these deaths and you will find that, a fire of undetermined origins, has been a factor in some way or other..."

Police Constable Shaw
RCMP Quarterly Magazine, 1961

PROLOGUE

Summer, 1909
Nahanni Valley
Northwest Territories, Canada

It was afternoon when search party pulled ashore on the stony beach and found weathered and withered remains of the two bodies. Both we're almost bleached bone, but there were still some shreds of decaying hair and flesh and remnants of worn tattered clothes, the elements having taken their toll. The first man was found lying on his back in the remaining scraps of his bedroll. The second man lay sprawled on the ground, tattered bedclothes still flapping in the slight breeze, one arm stretched in desperation towards a rusty bolt action rifle lying at the foot of a spruce tree a few yards away.

"THEY AIN'T GOT NO HEADS!" gasped one of the seven men who made up the party. Another searcher turned and wretched. The eerie horror mesmerized the rest of them. Duke Malloy grimaced and crouched down next to the body.

"Poole, what'd you make of this?"

Poole Field, a spare weathered ex-mountie turned prospector, came forward and knelt down on one knee next to Malloy. His sharp brown eyes examined the wound then he looked up at Malloy. "No animal did this. The head's been cut clean off."

"Yeah, the cut is clean," agreed Malloy pointing to the neck bones. "I've never seen anything like this Poole." He took a deep breath; his blue eyes scanned the sprawl of the valley's low grasslands and surrounding mountains. Their camp was located near a clump of spruce trees on a the gravelled left bank of the South Nahanni River near the outlet of what was later to be known as Headless Creek. It was the tattered flapping remains of the tent that had attracted the search party's attention.

"In fact, it doesn't look like any animals have scavenged these remains at all. Odd don't you think?" said Poole, looking up at Malloy. Their eyes met.

"Yeah, and that in itself is highly unusual," agreed Malloy. He turned to the other searchers. "Look around. See if you can find the skulls."

The men slowly backed away, their eyes darting all over.

They could feel it too thought Malloy. We're not alone.

Malloy, a Royal Canadian Mounted Police constable, had agreed to accompany this unofficial search party. Personally, Malloy had not put much stock in finding Frank and Willie MacLeod alive. Both brothers had set out three years ago to find the legendary valley of gold hidden in the Nahanni wilds. A third man named Wilkinson had supposedly accompanied them. The Nahanni bush was uncivilized; few men had ventured this far.

The MacLeod boys had made an earlier trip up the Nahanni in 1904 and had set up a placer mine in Flat River Canyon. That venture had proved unsuccessful. A year later, very determined to strike it rich; Willie and Frank decided to try their luck again. Their brother Charlie elected to stay behind. He'd had enough wild goose chases.

Charlie Macleod dropped his knapsack next to Field. He had dreaded this moment. He figured they were dead, but coming to terms with the actuality was something else. His stomach dropped; he felt queasy. His breath seemed to leave him for a moment. "This is Willie and Frank."

"Hey, Charlie, Poole, Duke, come look at this," called one of the other searchers.

"What is it Joe?" Asked Charlie.

Joe came forward. He was a solidly built man in his forties and dressed in dungarees and a black and white checked flannel shirt. In his right hand was a piece of wood. Duke took it from him. Charlie leaned over and read it. Someone had written on it: "We have found a fine prospect." Charlie shook his head. "They always claimed they'd strike it rich. But if they did, where's the gold?"

"Didn't you say there was another man with them?" said Malloy.

"Yeah, a Scottish feller named Wilkes or Wilkinson."

"Look around for another body," ordered Field.

Hours later the men sat around a fire where a pot of hot sweet tea was boiling. Their search had failed to find Wilkinson's body, or the heads of Willie and Frank MacLeod.

"Odd, nothing was stolen," remarked Malloy as he leaned over to grab the pot with a rag. He poured tea for the others, then himself.

"Yes," agreed Poole, his eyes surveying the surrounding forested mountains. "Any man, even a murderer, would need every bit of supplies he could take if he wanted to escape unaided."

"Even then he'd have a tough time of it," said Malloy

Well, I guess we'd better load the bodies up. I don't think any of us want to camp here tonight." Field glanced at Charlie MacLeod.

MacLeod said nothing, just stared at the swirling waters of the Nahanni River. Deadman's Valley, or Headless Valley as it later became known in the press, had claimed its first known victims. His brothers. Others would follow.

CHAPTER ONE: ANNETTE

Fort Simpson, N.W.T
June 1937

Duke Malloy cried out. His feet kicked off the blankets from him and his naked companion. Malloy opened his eyes and stared up at the log ceiling. His heart was pounding and he was sweating heavily. He ran a hand over his face and took a deep breath. He rolled onto his side and stared into the dark shadows of his cabin. He'd had the damn dream again. The war had been over for eighteen years, but the ghost of Tommy Birk came back to haunt him.

Tommy Birk had been a wide-eyed kid from Thunder Bay. He joined the fight against the Huns for a chance to leave the small northern Ontario town in search of adventure and glory. Tommy got more than he bargained for. Malloy, an older, more experienced recruit, had taken Tommy under his wing. The two men became good friends. Malloy had promised Tommy that one their first leave together; he would introduce Tommy to the pleasures of Madame Rose (there was an abundance of Madam Roses') and her house of ill repute in Paris. Tommy had been anxious to lose his virginity. But instead, he lost his life.

Vimy Ridge happened. Military strategy hadn't matured as quickly as the technology. The two sides stood slogging it out in the trenches like prehistoric cavemen, only their clubs were pounding artillery, mists of poison gas, and the staccato roar of machine guns. When it was over, and the trenches were filled with bodies and rivers of blood, Tommy Birk lay dead. His body was riddled with machine gun bullets. He looked like a chewed up rag doll.

Malloy had been wounded in the thigh. Thankfully he was treated before gangrene set in. The horror of war stayed with Malloy. The nightmares of blood and death, especially Tommy's, still haunted him. He had survived when so many of his comrades had not.

After the war, disillusioned, Duncan 'Duke' Malloy returned to Canada, and retreated back to Fort Simpson to spend quiet years hunting, trapping and prospecting. For here was a world he understood, knew and loved -- and a place that was isolated from the world's craziness.

A cool dry hand pressed against Malloy's cheek. In the dim early morning light that crept into his bedroom, he focused his grey eyes on the pretty, raven-haired round face of Rose Deerfoot. Malloy's shuddering breath inhaled the cabin reek of stale tobacco, old booze and human sweat.

"You were dreaming again," she said.

"I know." Malloy coughed and stretched out his right hand for the bottle of Canadian Four Star Whiskey that usually sat on the apple box nightstand next to his bed.

"It's empty, Duke. I threw it out."

Malloy groaned. "Where's my pipe`?"

Rose sighed. Such a waste. There was so much of life to enjoy; yet Duke Malloy preferred to wallow in self-pity. He wasn't so different from many of her people. At times she wondered why she still came to him. Perhaps it was her childhood memories of the brave Mountie who had rescued her father from a pack of wolves. Charlie Deerfoot had been treed for two days by a wolf pack while trapping. Then Malloy showed up. Charlie owed Malloy his life. Her father never let Rose forget that. There were times when on patrol Malloy would visit them and have a cup of tea and tell stories of what he had seen and heard. He was always smiling and carefree. He never forgot Rose; he was always bringing candy or flowers, and once Malloy even gave her a doll that he had bought for her in Dawson.

And now, that same handsome Mountie was a middle-aged man whose black hair was turning grey, whose slim, broad-shouldered frame was filling out, but not so much, smiled Rose. It was his eyes. Once warm and caring now they were cold and as hard as granite, his mouth a tight slit in his wind roughened lined face.

At the unexpected knock at the door, Rose quickly scampered out of bed. Naked, she crossed the room to pull on Malloy's housecoat. Malloy ran his fingers through his curly tangled hair and searched around for his pants. He found them hanging over the old wooden captain's chair in the corner. He struggled out of bed and into his pants. The knock at the door came again. More insistent.

"Coming," he wheezed, grimacing as his bare feet slapped across the cold wood floor. "Better make some coffee," he said to Rose.

Silently Rose went to the kitchen sink and began to rinse out the pot. Malloy opened the door, wondering who it could be. He rarely received visitors.

Standing on the small porch were a man and a girl. It was the girl that caught his eye. No, that wasn't right. She wasn't a girl; she was a woman. A small, well dressed woman whose attire was totally out of place for this desolate country. Bits of mud clung to the bottom of her tweed skirt. Malloy estimated her to be around 5'2" and 112 pounds. The man, 5'7", 160 pounds, was dressed in an expensive suit looking a bit worse for well also, with bits of mud caked onto the cuffs of his trousers and edges of his shoes. He looked to be in his late twenties or early thirties with brown hair and dark brown eyes. There was a feeling of sophistication and superiority. All this Malloy took in, his police training taking over his slightly inebriated senses. Malloy returned his attention to the woman.

"Mr. Duncan Malloy?" The woman looked questioningly at him.

"That's right, though folks around here call me Duke."

"Duke, eh," smirked the man.

"That's right." There was something damn irritating about the man thought Malloy. He wanted to smack him.

"My name is Annette Bouchard. This is my fiancé Mr. Henry David Colton."

"Pleased to meet you," he half-lied. A cool breeze swept into the cabin. Bits of loose paper fluttered around the rough floor. Malloy stared at his guests. "Well now, it's a bit crisp. Guess you'd better come in if you're gonna speak your peace. Sorry about the place, I don't usually have company. In fact, I just got up."

They entered Malloy's cabin, their eyes surveying the small, decrepit one room living quarters. Annette's attention riveted on Rose. Rose returned the attention with a bland stare. Henry grimaced at the rustic interior and sniffed at the smell of stale liquor and tobacco that pervaded the cabin. The thought of living in such filth turned his stomach.

"Please, sit down Miss Bouchard," gestured Malloy.

Colton pulled out his handkerchief and dusted off the wooden Captain's Chair. "Here darling."

Malloy pulled up an empty apple crate. "Here's a seat for you Mr. Colton."

"Thank you, I think I'll stand."

"Suit yourself. Now, Miss Bouchard, what brings a lady like yourself up here and see the likes of me?"

Annette Bouchard unbuttoned her coat and took off her hat. Malloy noticed how attractive she was. Her auburn hair cascaded down to her shoulders. Her eyes were the most violet Malloy had ever seen. She had a small straight nose and a wide mouth. Her body was petite but well proportioned, that even her tweed suit couldn't hide. Her voice was soft and pleasant. "I need a guide Mr. Malloy. We were told you that you sometimes hired out as a guide. I want you to take us to Headless Valley."

Malloy eyed his visitors. "Don't tell me, you're looking for the old MacLeod Boy's mine."

"You know of it?" Annette's eyes brightened.

Malloy laughed, choked on the laugh and coughed up a glob of phlegm, which he politely spit into the rag of handkerchief that had been stuffed into his pants pocket. "Miss, everybody 'round here knows about the McLeod's. Shoot, it ain't no secret. Why old Redpants, that's Albert Faille, goes out every summer lookin' for the lost mine. Then there's all the greenhorns. A few years ago a whole bunch of folks come out to prospect. Most of 'em gave up and went home. Some got killed. It's wild country in the bush, and no place for a city lady like yourself."

Annette Bouchard's violet eyes darkened. "You don't approve of women?"

Malloy grinned. "Sure I do-- in their own place. But this isn't some groomed park. It's a hard life here. It takes special woman to survive up here, and those that do, don't go trampin' around the bush."

"Does that mean you won't help us?" Asked Colton.

Malloy raised his eyes. "I didn't say that. Fact is I haven't given it any thought just yet. Hell, I just got up. Uh, beggin' your pardon ma'am...guess I'm not used to polite conversation. No, I was just givin' my opinion to your fiancée. But it ain't gonna be no piece of cake. Do you really want her to do this?"

"Mr. Colton doesn't have a choice in the matter. It's my expedition," interrupted Annette.

"I've been trying to persuade her otherwise," said Colton.

"So I see." Malloy sat down on the bed as Rose brought coffee to Annette and Colton. Both accepted. Rose poured a mug for Malloy and brought it too him, then sat on the bed next to him.

"Tell me, what's so special about you finding the mine. It's more than that, isn't it?" prompted Malloy.

"If I find the mine, I believe I'll find my father- George Bouchard and brother Andre Mr. Malloy," stated Annette. She took a sip of coffee and grimaced. Annette placed the cup on the saucer. "They came up here two years ago."

"So did a lot of other people. They found nothing. What makes you think your father and brother found anything either?" replied Malloy.

"Because of the man they went with. He told them he knew where there was a whole valley of gold."

Malloy shook off the doziness. His back stiffened. "What was this fellow's name?"

"A Mr. Williams. He was a tall, Scottish gentleman. White hair. Very distinguishing."

Malloy began thinking. Williams could be an alias for Wilkinson or Wilkes, the name of the man that went with Willie and

Frank. A bulletin had been put out for him at the time of the murder, but he was never found. There were reports that he had been seen in Vancouver with five thousand dollars. Local gossip alluded to the fact that the man probably had headed south into California. Nothing had ever been confirmed. The murderer of Willie and Frank MacLeod had never been found. Charlie had convinced himself that a bear had gotten his brothers. But Malloy knew better. He had seen the marks with his own eyes. He turned his attention back to his guests. "You say your brother and father came up here. When was that?"

"Two years ago," replied Annette.

"What does your father do for a living?" Asked Malloy.

"He used to be an investment counsellor and stockbroker, but when the stock market crashed so did his business. To support us, he took lot of odd jobs. A few years ago, Father managed to secure a job with the Bank of Montreal as a bank teller, but he wasn't really satisfied. We had been quite wealthy once, and Father hoped we would again. My brother Andre had to quit school when Father lost the business. He worked at a variety of jobs helping to support us."

"I see." Malloy took a sip of his coffee. He refrained from making a face in front of his guests. Rose made lousy coffee. "You're from Quebec?"

"Montreal."

"And how did your father meet this Mr. Williams?" asked Malloy. God he needed a smoke. Now where had he left his pipe?

"Father met Mr. Williams at some club he attended with a friend of his." Annette smiled. "That's when I met Henry."

Malloy shifted his gaze to Colton. "Is that so?"

Colton turned to Anne. "I don't think Mr. Malloy need hear about our romance."

"And what do you do Mr. Colton?"

"I come from an old San Francisco family. We have interests in banks and investments such as real estate and insurance. I happened to have been in Montreal on family business when Annette and I met. Why do you ask?"

"Just curious." Malloy smiled. "Can I get you some more coffee?" He gulped the last of drips from his cup.

"None for me thank you," said Anne. She hadn't touched a drop. She placed the cup on an apple crate that doubled as a nightstand next to the bed.

"I've had my fill," spat Colton.

Malloy reached into his jacket that hung on the post of his bed and pulled out his pipe and tobacco. "Two years is a long time Miss Bouchard. Like I told you, there was a bit of a gold rush of sorts around here at that time. Lot of greenhorns came out from down East. Normally it'd be hard to pick up a trail that cold, but you may have a chance." Malloy paused as he lit his pipe and took a couple of puffs. His hands steadied. "Since I know what your father was after, I know which area they'd be heading into."

Annette's eyes lit up. "When can we leave?"

"Now hold on," said Malloy. "I haven't even decided if I want to take you. That area is known as Headless Valley, and beyond is very rugged bush country. There are no real maps. As I said before, it's not a place for a lady like yourself."

"But if my father and brother are there, I must go."

"I can understand your feelings, but it is very likely that they're not alive. They weren't experienced woodsmen. The likelihood of them surviving a winter, let alone two winters out there is damn near impossible."

"Have you heard Mr. Malloy? Now will you stop this foolishness Annette?" said Colton. He turned to Malloy. "I have tried in everyway to persuade her otherwise Mr. Malloy. She's very stubborn."

"So I see," said Malloy, turning his attention back to Annette. "Now the best thing for you to do is go back home. Maybe if I feel so inclined, I could have a bit of a look and let you know if I find anything."

Annette Bouchard shook her head defiantly. "No. I will go on this search with or without you. That is my Father and brother out there." Annette turned to Colton. "Have I made myself clear?"

Colton shrugged and looked at Malloy. Malloy shook his head. What in hell's name was he getting himself into? Did he really want to go gallivanting off into the bush on a fruitless search? And there was something about Colton that Malloy didn't like. As a Mountie, he'd had years of experience sizing people up. If he went on this expedition, he'd have to trust this couple, just as much as they would have to trust him. They'd have to watch each others' backs. It was dangerous in the bush. And though he didn't know anything about Colton, there was a nagging trigger tapping in his head. Not to mention the fact that they were tenderfeet. Inexperience alone would get you crippled or killed out there, which was just the same thing. Mind you, they looked rich. Colton looked like he was well-heeled. He could take them to Headless Valley. The trip there would probably cure them of any exploration fever. He'd make some money, come back, sit on his ass and get drunk. On the other hand, curiosity gnawed at him. He'd always want to solve the MacLeod case, and there had been a number of other unsolved murders in Headless Valley. He'd always felt they

17

were linked. But he was old now. He hadn't been out in the bush for a while, not since last trapping season. He was comfortable here. But liquor money was scarce. Ah, hell... his life wasn't worth much anyway, and there's nothing like an old fool. Malloy stared into Annette's eyes and drank deeply from those violet pools. He felt instantly aroused. Shit, she was old enough to be his daughter. He shook his head, took a deep breath and coughed. "Okay Miss Bouchard, you win. But there's a lot of preparations to make, and not much time. It's already June. We only have until late August before the weather is going to start turning nasty. It's a three-week journey to Headless Valley from here. And to go beyond, well, that depends on a lot of other things."

"What about flying in?" asked Colton?

Malloy looked at the young man. "There was a fellow name of Doc Oaks that flew up there, I think in '28 with a pilot out of Fort Simpson. They landed near the MacLeod's placer mine. So it's been done. But pilots are scarce this time of year and they cost money. You financing this expedition Mr. Colton?"

Annette looked at Henry. Henry frowned, and then said, "I suppose you could say that. Flying would save time."

"Okay," said Malloy, "let me make some inquiries. You folks staying at the hotel?"

"Yes." Answered Annette.

"I'll come by tomorrow with a list of supplies," said Malloy to Colton.

"You can look it over and okay it. You can get everything at the Hudson Bay store. By the way Miss Bouchard, have you got a picture of your father or brother?"

"Certainly, why?"

"I'd like to borrow it. Maybe, some folks saw them. It might help our search."

Annette spent a few moments searching the contents of her purse. She pulled out two small snapshots. The first picture was of Annette's father. It was a portrait head shot showing a dapper round faced man with a cleft chin and neatly combed dark hair. A short trimmed moustache fell below a patrician nose. The second picture showed two men, Annette's father and her brother, a serious dark haired looking young man in his twenties. Both we decked out in dark suits, vests and ties.

"Thank you. I'll see you get them back." He glanced at the photos, and then laid them on his bed.

Annette stood up. "Then I guess everything is arranged. Good-bye Mr. Malloy. We'll see you tomorrow. Come, Henry."

Malloy stood up. Rose opened the door for their departing guests.

"Til tomorrow Mr. Malloy," said Colton with a nod.

Malloy waved. "Tomorrow."

After they left, Rose said, "You're going to do this? It is dangerous. I don't trust that man Colton. You could get yourself killed."

Malloy shrugged. "If I don't, that girl will do it alone, and she and her fiancé will die. At least with me they have a chance. There's nothing else to do around here. Besides, I could use the money."

"Pah. You don't need money. All you do is buy whiskey. You do it for the girl. I saw you look her. She's nice. Young. Pretty. That's why you do it. You're an old fool. I don't know why I put up with you. Maybe I find myself a nice buck."

"You're jealous," laughed Malloy.

Rose punched him in the arm and glared at him. "The mountains are death. Do you so much want to join the Great Spirit? I know there's a sickness in your heart. Ever since you come back, you are different. I see you die slowly."

"We all grow old. Dreams die. I haven't got a lot left. I've nothing to lose," said Malloy.

Rose moved close to him and grasped his arms. "You are a good man Duke Malloy. I care about you. But you are crazy sometimes."

"Yeah." Malloy looked into her face. Character lines were already etching their way around her eyes and mouth. Rose would be old before her time. The hard life aged the young quickly here. Malloy thought of Annette as he untied Rose's robe. It fell open, revealing Rose's young, round soft breasts. He grasped them in his hands, bent over her and kissed them. He sucked her nipples and felt them harden. Her breath quickens. She undid his pants. A little nudge and they dropped around his ankles. Malloy pushed Rose back onto the bed.

CHAPTER TWO: FACT AND LEGEND

Constable Claude Marchand of the Royal Canadian Mounted Police sat in a wooden armchair with his feet propped up on an old battered wooden desk. He peered up from his March issue of LIFE magazine as Duke Malloy thumped into the sparse, but functional R.C.M.P. post, which consisted of a small outer office, a jail and barracks. "Hear you got a guide job for some greenhorns," he said.

"Yeah, news sure travels fast," remarked Malloy. He pulled up a straight back wooden chair and sat across the desk from Marchand.

Constable Claude Marchand was a burly pink-faced man in his thirties. He had short thinning brown hair and a wispy moustache. His uniform was wrinkled, as if he'd slept in it. His boots were dusty and scuffed. Marchand had been stationed in Fort Simpson for two years. He had a reputation of being fair, open-minded and good-natured--when sober.

The Mountie detachment, established at Fort Simpson in 1912, normally consisted of 9 men; but the Inspector was at a meeting in Yellowknife and the balance of the force was out on patrol. With the growing concern about the war in Europe, and threats of Nazi sabotage, the responsibility of securing borders was becoming more important.

"Well, doze two du ben lookin' all over town for you. I understan' dat dere searchin' for du old MacLeod mine." Marchand shook his head. "People, dey sure is crazy."

"Not all the time," replied Malloy. "The woman's father and brother got lost looking for the mine. She thinks if she finds the mine, she'll find them. They came up here two years ago." Malloy handed Marchand the pictures Annette had loaned him.

Marchand glanced at the pictures. "Dere probably dead." Marchand stood up. "Get you some coffee?"

"Sure." Malloy took the pictures back. "Did the woman ask the force for help?"

"Not dat I know of. We haven't du manpower to launch a search for men dat been missing two year. You know what leading a search party up dat Nahanni is like." Marchand poured two mugs of coffee from a pot that rested on an old black stove in a corner of the office. He put sugar and cream in his. He knew Malloy drank his coffee black.

"Well, there's always a chance they might be alive. There was a man with them. You remember the MacLeod story?"

"Who don't 'round here, eh?" Said Marchand as he sipped his coffee.

"You remember about a third fellow named Wilkes or Wilkinson who went with the MacLeod's?"

"You mean dat?" Marchand's jaw dropped.

Malloy didn't let him finish. "There was a Scotsman with Miss Bouchard's father and brother. Supposedly his name is Williams."

Marchand drained his mug. "You find anyting, you let me know. Unnerstand?"

"Sure," replied Malloy and he finished his coffee. "But I want a favor in return."

Marchand looked suspiciously at Malloy. "You go to hell Malloy. I know all about your favors. What is it?"

"Can you run a check on a man named Henry David Colton from San Francisco?"

"What's dis guy done?" Asked Marchand.

"I don't know yet," replied Malloy.

"It will take some time. I doubt I have it before you leave on your expedition. You leaving soon?"

"It's already June. We have to. But let me know, whenever." Malloy got up. "And now, well, some of us have work to do."

"Work? You? Dat's da funnest ting I ever hear," jeered Marchand. "Ah, get de hell outta here."

Annette Bouchard sat on the bed. She held a mirror in her left hand and brushed her hair with her right. The hotel room was dusty, dingy and austere, but there wasn't any other choice. Fort Simpson only had one hotel. The problem was it reminded her of home. Her father had been a prominent banker and financier until the crash. They had rubbed elbows with the rich and the infamous of Montreal, New York and Toronto. And then, her father had lost it all. Annette remembered her father when he had come home that day. She had never seen him cry before. His face was withdrawn and dark. His shoulders, usually straight were slumped. She remembered how quietly he had entered their home and had whispered to Mama, "It's over. We're through. It's all gone."

Though father tried to pretend that everything was all right, whatever savings they had seemed to vanish quickly, as well as Mama's jewellery, including her wedding ring with the four-carat diamond. The house was sold and they moved into a dingy three-bedroom apartment. Father swallowed his pride and pounded the streets looking for work, finally getting a job as a bank clerk. Tears came to Annette's eyes as she remembered her father coming home from work. His proud stride, replaced by a shuffle; his straight back, slouched; his youthful appearance aged with worry. And then, one day he entered through the door like his old self. Hope renewed him. He told Mama and the family that he had to go away, but when he came back, everything was going to be as it had been before. Once again, they'd be living, travelling, and dining in style. Naturally Annette's brother, Andre insisted on accompanying Father. A nasty argument ensued between Father and Andre. Shouting quaked the walls. Father didn't want the women to be alone; but in the end, Andre won. And now, they're both gone. Mama was never the same. All the stress and change had been too much for her. She sat silently in a dark room, not speaking, not caring. It was then Annette knew that it was up to her to find her father and her brother Andre and bring them home. Leaving her mother in the care of her cousins, she snatched Colton and headed west.

Annette's thoughts jumped to Duke Malloy. She had been told he was an ex-Mountie. But those fantasies of the strong proud policeman exploded when she had met him. It was obvious he'd been quite handsome in his youth, but now, he was nothing more than an unwashed, unshaven drunkard, a man who had obviously given up on life. What had happened to him? She also wondered what he saw in that Indian girl and she with him. She was obviously a lot younger than he. The idea of the two of them together repulsed her. Yet, she had been told that he was a good guide. He knew the land and how to survive in it. She hoped she had made the right choice. Her life depended on it.

There was a knock at her door. Annette lay down the brush and mirror and wrapped her housecoat more securely as she stood up and went to the door.

"Who's there?"

"Henry," answered a familiar voice from the other side.

Annette opened the door.

"I thought you'd be dressed," said Henry as he entered.

"It takes me a little longer to get ready. Have you seen Mr. Malloy?" asked Annette.

"That drunk," sniffed Henry, "I was embarrassed yesterday. Going to see that man, living in such squalor. And that Indian woman was young enough to be his daughter. It was disgusting. We'd be better off without him. In fact, we'd be better off away from here. This is no place for you."

Annette took Henry's face in her hands. "We've been through all this before. I am going to find out what happened to my father and brother. They're all I have left since Mama died last year. Mr. Malloy is the only man around here who knows that territory. Now stop being so jealous."

"Jealous?" Henry removed Annette's hands from his face. "Of all the..."

"Knock, knock," boomed a voice from behind them.

They turned together.

"Uh, sorry. I didn't realize," said Malloy.

"What is it?" asked Henry.

"The supplies. I told you I'd be over in the morning." Malloy tipped his Stetson," Uh, good morning Miss Bouchard." His eyes drank in her shapely form.

Annette smiled. "Good morning Mr. Malloy, nice to see you. Henry, why don't you go downstairs with Mr. Malloy. I'll join you both in a few minutes."

Henry looked at her, and realized that his fiancée was wearing only nightclothes and standing barefoot in front of a strange man. He felt his face redden. "Excellent idea." He turned to Malloy. "Come Mr. Malloy."

Malloy was leaning against the doorpost. He winked at Annette, and then followed Colton.

As Henry Colton left Annette's room, he made a note to himself to discuss Annette's lack of discretion with her later.

Downstairs in the hotel cafe, Malloy and Colton ordered breakfast.

"Here's the list of supplies we'll need. The Hudson's Bay will have most of it, the rest you can pick up at one of trading posts. Oh, and I haven't been able to locate a bush pilot who's free to do charter. I tried a couple of the local air companies, but it seems they're all busy these days with the mail and all."

Colton took the list from Malloy and looked it over. We really need all this?" he asked.

"Mr. Colton, there ain't no stores out there. If you run out of supplies, it could mean your death. As it is, we haven't got a lot of time. It'll take us two to three weeks just to get to Deadman's Valley."

"Very well."

Gussy Johanssen, the cook and Café owner, brought their breakfasts. Malloy had ordered steak and eggs, toast, hash browns and coffee. Colton just had toast and coffee.

"That looks great. I'll have an order of the same," said Annette.

Both men looked up and rose while Annette sat.

Gussy smiled politely. "Sure thing Miss. It'll just be a minute. Coffee?"

"Yes, thank you."

"Are you sure you want all that food?" Asked Colton.

"I'm famished." Annette smiled at Malloy. "It must be the air up here."

Colton moodily picked up a piece of toast and took a bite.

"So, Mr. Malloy, when can we start?" Asked Annette.

Malloy put down his coffee cup. She looked beautiful this morning. Her auburn hair was combed and tied in back. She wore flannel slacks and a man's checked shirt, practical, not stylish. "As soon as your fiancé here buys the supplies. I just gave him a list. The boys at the store are already getting the stuff together."

Colton took a sip of his coffee and grimaced. The coffee tasted like boiled bitter dishwater. He put the cup down and reached for the sugar bowl. "I understand, from the hotel clerk that you were once a Mountie Mr. Malloy."

"That was before the war. I was there when the MacLeod brother's bodies were found. They were the first."

"The first?" Questioned Annette.

"The first of the bodies." Malloy began eating his steak while he talked. "There have been a number of mysterious deaths in the Nahanni, the last being Phil Powers."

"It's probably nothing more than backwoods superstitions," scoffed Colton." Surely wild animals must've got them."

Malloy looked across at Colton. "Mr. Colton, only ignorant men aren't afraid. I was there for some of the investigations, and I've taken part in the search parties. But the facts are plain and simple and so far the Mounties haven't been able to solve any of the murders."

Johanssen came back with Annette's breakfast. He set the plate down before her. "Good eating Miss."

"I'm just about to tell them about the legend of the Nahanni Gussy," said Malloy.

Johanssen looked at Annette and Henry. "Good, maybe it'll change their minds about looking for gold. No good has ever come of anyone who has. The wild men see to that. You'd do well to pay attention. Old Duke here knows. He's been out there."

"Well, come on with your ghost stories Malloy," taunted Colton.

Malloy finished his steak and sat back. He took a sip of coffee. "Since you asked so polite like, I will. Now eat your breakfasts and I'll tell you the legend of the Nahanni. The story begins years ago. I forget who it was who first told me about it; but the story goes that this Indian named Little Nahanni came out of the bush with gold nuggets, big as a man's fist. The Indian claimed to have come from a valley where winter could not touch the land. It's said that men who leave the soil of the Valley alone, go unharmed. Prospectors will be found dead. And that's pretty much been true. The McLeod brothers were the first in this century. We found their decapitated bodies at their camp on the Headless Creek. By 1909 some thirty prospectors have either died or disappeared while working the valley. Fellow named Martin Jorgensen was searching for the lost gold mine. Jorgensen was a good friend of old Poole Field, another ex-mountie and local prospector and trapper. He had even sent Poole a message to come quickly, claiming he had struck it rich. But Poole was too late. Poole found Jorgensen's remains. Jorgensen's cabin had been burnt to a crisp. He also found Jorgensen's gun. It was loaded and cocked, but Jorgensen never got the chance to use it. That was back in 1915. Old Poole told me about that when I came back from the war. In 1922 John O'Brien disappeared. His body was never found. Old Angus Hall was prospecting on the Flat River in '27. He bought it too. A few years back, in '32 Constable Martin found the remains of Phil Powers. Phil had a cabin at the mouth of Irvine Creek at Flat River. Powers too had been searching for the gold. Nothing left of Phil but a charred headless skeleton and a burnt out cabin. Whatever it was that got Phil, never gave him a chance to get to his gun. And just last year, Will Epler and Joe Mulholland disappeared. They had a place at Glacier Lake. A bush pilot named Dalziel found their cabin and store burnt to the ground.

"And to whom are these deaths attributed?" Asked Colton.

"At first the Indians were blamed. But the fact is that the local tribes around here are scared of the Nahanni valley. They won't venture into it. They claim Evil Spirits inhabit the region."

"What draws the men there?" Asked Annette. "I mean, so many men have died, why do more keep going there?"

Malloy smiled. "Gold, the legendary hidden valley of gold, and man's greed. Men travelled this area on their way up to the Klondike. As to the deaths, well as I said before, initially the Nahanni or Nah'aa Indians were blamed. It's a known fact that the Nah'aa Indians didn't like strangers; but smallpox wiped them out a number of years ago. Now other stories have it that great apes that were part of a shipwrecked Spanish Galleon's cargo moved inland are responsible for the killings; or maybe it was a band of white cannibals, remnants of that Spanish shipwreck that inhabit the Nahanni inland. Other Indian legends say that the Sasquatch, a mysterious half-man, half-ape creature, is responsible. And still another legend has it that there exists a tribe of wild men led by a mysterious white woman guard the Nahanni territory. Take your pick. Fact is we don't know what's out there, but a lot of good men have died under very mysterious circumstances. You might still want to reconsider."

"Refill your coffees?" Asked Johanssen. "Hey Duke, don't ferget to tell 'em about May."

"May?" Asked Annette.

"Yes, there's one woman who went missing. Even has a creek named after her," said Malloy. He sipped his coffee. "She was a cousin of Mary Field, that's Poole Field's wife. As I told you, he and I were on the expedition that found the McLeod brothers bodies. Anyway, it was back in '20. July it was. May had been staying with the Fields, but she was acting strange. Now all the men were out working trap lines. Anyway Poole gets a message that May is missing and nowhere in camp. Naturally a search was organized and they tracked her up Mary's River into the hills. Poole had five good hunters with him. May was travelling fast, barely stopping to rest. They found articles of her clothing along the way and it became obvious real fast that she was travelling stark naked. Now the mosquitoes and black flies are real thick and vicious in the bush. You can't survive long without clothing to protect you. They tracked her well into the rugged back country and up into the mountains. It seemed she was heading towards Simpson, which was her home. They followed her for nine days and lost her near the canyons around Deadman's Valley. Never a trace of her ever found."

"Of all the ridiculous things I've ever heard of," scoffed Colton. "What rubbish."

"Well Mr. Colton, I can't make a believer out of you; but as I said, the fact remains that people have died and disappeared there under mysterious circumstances. Even Doc Oaks when he flew in with Jack Hammill found remains near the MacLeod's old placer mind. That was around ten years ago."

"Any idea whose remains they were?" Asked Annette.

"Naw. There wasn't enough left to make any kind of identification. But even barring legends and murder, it's rugged country out there. One mistake can cost you your life. So, you still willing to go through with this?"

"Yes."

Malloy shook his head. "Well, I'll say this for you Miss Bouchard, you've got spunk." He grinned at her and downed his coffee.

CHAPTER THREE: DEADMAN'S VALLEY

Late June, 1937
Second Canyon
Nahanni Valley

"So this is it," said Annette. She looked around. Majestic Nahanni Butte was behind them. They stood on a stony beach leading to a low, lush green valley. The green lowlands gave way to heavy mixed forest. Jagged mountains thrusting granite fingers into the sky surrounded them. To the West, towering cliffs stood sentry.

"Deadman's Valley," said Malloy. "It was here, back in 1909 that we found Frank and Willie. Do you want to go ashore?" Malloy checked his pocket watch. "It's almost time for dinner anyway. That dark mountain you see over yonder is called Bald Mountain," pointed Malloy.

Colton looked at the deserted beach. He liked this trek less and less. He felt the hairs on the back of his neck prickle. Colton shook his head. This was ridiculous. There was nothing to be scared of, nothing here but trees, water and mountains. Yet there was a silence within the soft bird and inspect sounds, an ominous foreboding. Malloy steered the boat towards shore. Minutes later they jumped out, and pulled the boat onto the beach. Their boots crunched on the stony ground.

"We found the bodies over here," pointed Malloy, indicating a spot near the edge of some spruce trees. "One of the boys was lying in his bedroll. The other was sprawled forward trying to reach his gun. Never did find their heads, nor any sign of the other man with them."

"Do you think the man murdered the McLeod brothers?" Annette shuddered.

"No. The guns were left, as were the remains of their supplies. I think they were attacked and this fellow Wilkinson ran off. Probably died in the bush. The question is, what attacked them. We found no other marks around. Area was swept clean."

"What about the other victims you told us about?" asked Annette?

"Again, no clues as far as I know. Fire wiped out any evidence."

"Must you talk about such gruesome matter," said Colton. He scanned the surrounding mountains. "This whole area sends chills down my spine. I feel like we're being watched."

"For a sceptical tenderfoot like yourself, I'm surprised," said Malloy. "But your reactions are normal. Anyone whose come down this way feels the same. Let's have some dinner and push on. It's a long trek and we've a good number of hours ahead of us."

Henry David Colton slapped the mosquito at the back of his neck and glared at Malloy and Annette. They sat in the bow of the boat, talking. They'd been on the river a week, with the towering scarred and jagged cliffs staring down at them. They'd travelled through the steep walled second canyon and had passed into the third canyon. The days were hot and humid; the nights were cold. It'd been gruelling work paddling in the swirling waters and making portage on land with the boat at the more treacherous intervals. The brush was thick, and thorns tore at their clothes. Flies buzzed around them like ambushing aircraft. Malloy's muscles had screamed, it'd been months since he'd been in the bush. He felt the thirst for booze, and had managed to sneak a few shots each night to keep him going. But the black flies and mosquitoes were worse. Nothing would discourage them from taking their pound of flesh. There were some parts that Malloy said he could have traversed in the water if not for the inexperienced 'crew'. Colton was tired, bug bitten and sunburnt. He was sick of Malloy berating him. The first night he forgot to hoist their food up from a tree to keep the animals away from it. Some small animals had gotten into the crackers and flour. Malloy had roared a piece of flesh off his back, embarrassing him in front of Annette; but worst of all, Annette seemed more enthralled with Malloy than with him. At night around the campfire, Malloy spun tales of his days with the Royal Canadian Mounted Police and the horror of the trenches. Colton couldn't understand what attracted Annette to Malloy. Malloy was a middle-aged, drunken has-been, though Colton had to admit that he hadn't seen Malloy take a drop since they'd started out. Probably drank at night when he and Annette were asleep he thought. Colton fumed inside. He'd paid for everything so far, and all he'd received was a brief thanks and a kiss.

"Say, what's that roar?" asked Colton.

Malloy looked up. "We're getting close to Hell's Gate. We should find a spot to land. We won't be able to go up the rapids; we'll have to portage. Be on the lookout for whirlpools. The water's gonna get rough."

Colton looked out. The river was moving faster now. White-capped waves punched the boat. It rocked and rolled down the river. Water splashed over the sides. Colton clutched the bow. His stomach did a loop de loop. Lunch came up to greet him. He leaned over the side and spewed.

Malloy gunned the 4 h.p. Johnson outboard and guided the boat towards the shore. It was like riding a bucking bronco. Water soaked them.

"Is there anything I can do?" asked Annette. Her wet shirt clung to her breasts.

Malloy stared at her for a moment, then quickly turned his eyes elsewhere and shook his head. He could feel the tension as the small engine battled for their survival. A whirlpool bore to his left. He gunned the engine, and prayed they wouldn't run out of gas. He'd been filling the engine every hour. The water was sucking them back into its waiting arms. "Break out the paddles."

Annette reached down and untied the paddles from the sides of the boat. She passed one to Colton. "Henry!"

Colton looked up and wiped his mouth. He clutched the paddle and stabbed the water.

Malloy shook his head. Their technique was lousy, but it seemed to help. Slowly they pulled toward shore.

Twenty-five minutes later Malloy jumped out and dragged the boat onto the beach in a small cove near Hell's Gate. Annette and Henry, totally exhausted, lay in the boat.

"All ashore. We'll make camp here and portage tomorrow. Colton, see if you can find some dry wood for a fire. I'll set up the tents," said Malloy.

Colton groaned. He ached in places he didn't know he could ache in. His arms were like leaden anchors. Slowly he pushed himself up.

Malloy emptied the boat and watched Colton lurch into the forest. He smiled to himself. Malloy turned the boat over and tied it down. He unpacked the tents and set them up.

Annette dug into her pack and pulled out dry clothes. Malloy watched her stagger into the bush. "Don't go too far. Never know what you'll meet out there. And stay away from poison ivy."

"I promise to be careful Mr. Malloy, but really, you can't expect a girl to change on an open beach." She laughed and disappeared into the bush.

"Is this enough?" asked Colton.

Malloy looked up. Colton had dragged in a cracked limb. "Looks a little green. We need dry, old wood. Lots of small pieces."

Colton dropped the log. He glared at Malloy, turned and tromped back into the bush. Malloy shook his head and chuckled.

Dinner was a simple fare of bannock, pork and beans and tea. Annette thought it was better than any restaurant. The fire crackled merrily. Colton, too tired to eat, fell asleep.

"Poor Henry." said Annette. "He really isn't up to all this."

"I wasn't either when I first came out here," said Malloy, "But you either toughen up, leave or die." He looked up at the tree-covered mountains. The sun was setting and the light on the river accented the violent eddies and whirlpools. The river swirled with ever-changing texture.

"Why'd you come here?" asked Annette.

Malloy stared into the fire. "Peace of mind. That's why I came back. When you look around and see the beauty here, you realize you're in God's country. It also let's you know how small and insignificant you are in the scheme of things."

"You don't think my father and brother are alive do you," said Annette, changing subjects. She'd noticed how moody Malloy got when he was introspective. She worried about him. Better to get him thinking about the problem at hand.

Malloy took his pipe out. "No I don't. I've been on too many search parties."

A low vibrating roar soared from Henry's tent.

Annette smiled. "Henry's a dear. When I told him about my search, he insisted he come along. He's never camped. His father and mother separated when he was a boy. He was raised in a house full of women."

"What did his father do?" asked Malloy.

"Land speculation, investments I gather. His mother comes from old money. Henry doesn't talk much about his family. I did meet his mother. She's very aristocratic, but nice."

Malloy puffed on his pipe. A wolf howled in the distance. "We'd best turn in. We've got a rough trip ahead and we'll need our rest."

Annette sighed. "It's just so beautiful out here." She looked up at the flickering stars.

Malloy stood up. "Well, don't stay up too late."

Annette watched Malloy. It was comforting, having him here. She poured herself a cup of tea and watched sparks shoot up from the dying crackling embers, like tiny rockets on Victoria Day. It was so peaceful. Somewhere out here was her father and brother, and she would find them --even if they were dead. The least she could do was give them a Christian burial.

Several twigs snapped. Annette leaped up and turned around. Two glowing eyes peered out from the bushes. The hairs on her neck prickled.　Her cup plummeted to ground.　The bushes shook and moved.　A huge grizzly bear walked into the campsite.　He stopped, stood on his hind legs and roared.　She screamed.

CHAPTER FOUR: BEYOND HELL'S GATE

Malloy bolted upright at the scream. He clutched his .455 Colt Service revolver in his right hand and his Lee-Metford .303 bolt-action rifle in his left. Charging out of his tent Malloy staggered to a halt, not helping to notice the giant Grizzly rearing up just a few feet in front of him. It stood seven and half feet tall on its hind legs and must've weighed at least one thousand pounds. Malloy had seen the human remains of a Grizzly attack; being a victim was far from a cherished thought. He also knew many a trapper who wore the scars of a Grizzly attack, and for some, death would've been kinder. One swipe from a Grizzly's paw could tear a limb or a head from a man's body. Malloy fired his pistol sending a bullet skimming over the grizzly's head. It roared and turned. He jammed the pistol into his long johns, aimed the rifle and fired. Blood and bits of fur exploded from the bear's right shoulder. Bad shot. The only way to kill a Grizzly was to shoot it between the eyes. If you were a bad shot, a bullet into the left shoulder near the heart would slow the bear down and give you time for a second death shot. But that was the only chance you got. The Grizzly charged. Malloy fired again then rolled aside as the Grizzly sideswiped him, knocking Malloy flat on his ass, and crashing into the tent. Malloy fired four times into the rolling, thrashing mass of fur and canvas. His rifle was empty. He tossed it aside, picked himself up and drew the Colt.

Annette took a step forward. "Thank God."

"Stay back!" warned Malloy, "He might be still alive."

A painful roar shook the forest. The Grizzly rose like a phoenix from the torn remnants of the tent. Blood stained its fur. Malloy fired the remaining five shots into the Grizzly's head. Blood and bone spewed forth. Then like Goliath hit by David's stone, it crashed at Malloy's feet.

Malloy stepped back and took a deep breath. His chest heaved. His hands trembled. Malloy crept around the carcass and rummaged through his scattered belongings until he found his ammunition belt. His breathing didn't return to normal until both the pistol and rifle were reloaded.

Colton's popped out of his tent. "What's all the ruckus?"

Annette looked at Malloy. They both broke up laughing. Then Malloy's face-hardened as he looked at Colton.

"Did you put the supplies up tonight?" Malloy asked Colton.

Colton shrugged. "I was too tired. I just stashed them in a tent."

Malloy took a couple of steps towards Colton. "Y'know bears," he thumbed towards the Grizzly's carcass, "they can't see worth a damn, but their noses, they smell real good with 'em. Maybe you should try using yours."

Malloy's fist crashed into Henry's face. Henry's head snapped sideways and his feet lifted off the ground as he flew backwards. "You stupid sonofabtich," roared Malloy," you're carelessness almost killed Annette, not to mention me!"

Colton skidded to a stop in the dirt. He groaned and shook his head. Blood poured from his bruised nose. He sat up and brushed himself off, then with a cry and fists flying, Colton charged Malloy. Malloy sidestepped Colton and tapped him with an elbow on the back of the neck. Colton crashed to the ground, dust flying into his open mouth. He coughed and rolled over. He wiped the blood from a cut on his lip.

"Had enough?" asked Malloy.

"Bastard!" muttered Colton. He leaped up and punched Malloy.

The blow pressed into Malloy's stomach. Malloy grunted, but remained unaffected. Colton staggered back. His jaw dropped. "Uh-oh."

Malloy backhanded Colton with his right fist. Colton flew sideways and hit the ground. He groaned and lay still.

"Enough! Both of you!" screamed Annette. "Henry, what's gotten into you? And you," she said turning to Malloy, "you should know better. You're just like children."

Malloy grinned sheepishly. Annette tried to be angry. She knew Malloy was right. Colton's carelessness and naivety could get them killed. "I'm sorry."

Annette helped Henry up. "Let's have a look at you. Come into the tent, I'll clean you up."

Colton glared at Malloy as Annette led him to his tent. "I'll get you," he mouthed.

Malloy merely nodded at him. Then he turned his attention to his tent. It was beyond repair. He went through the ruins and collected his belongings and supplies. With an axe in his hand Malloy went into the bush and cut three long branches. He made a simple frame and using the remains of canvass from his tent made a basic shelter. Squatting down by the riverbank, he cleaned himself off. Annette padded over to him.

"I'm sorry for all the trouble Henry caused."

Malloy nodded. "How's he doing?"

Annette smiled, "His nose and lip is red and swollen, jaw's going to be a bit sore but he'll live."

"Stupidity out here can get you killed," said Malloy.

"He knows. He just been so ---"

"Jealous?"

Annette lowered her eyes. "Yes. But there seems to be something else. I've never seen him like this, so grim. It's not like him at all."

"The wilds test a man. Some don't like what they see in themselves. But as long as he keeps sensible, everything should be all right." Malloy stood and put his arm around Annette's shoulder. She leaned into him. "Now you go and get some sleep. We got a long day tomorrow."

"Okay. Good night Mr. Malloy."

"Duke."

"Duke." she smiled.

A bald eagle swooped over them like a silent warplane, and then soared down the canyon. The menacing jagged rock cliffs glared down at them like stern sentinels from either side as the river narrowed. On their left a rocky pillar, known as Pulpit Rock, jutted out from the cliff, and marked the passing of Hell's Gate. The kicker whined in protest as it struggled upstream against the turbulent waters. The sun, a blazing signal, was just beginning to burn off the early morning mist. Tall, scarred, forested cliffs formed formidable walls on either side of the river. Annette felt that she was truly in God's country or maybe it was more aptly the devils'. The wild untamed landscape was magnificent. Already she had seen a Dal sheep and some elk. Annette took a deep breath and shivered. She pulled the collar up on her wool jacket. Henry sat in front of her, his face like carved granite. He was barely civil this morning. Henry had never showed anything but contempt for Malloy. This morning had been no different. And he had barely acknowledged Annette. She knew he was jealous. But how could he be jealous of a middle-aged man? Yet, Annette also knew that she was attracted to Malloy. He wasn't bad looking, but it was something else. He had changed since they started out. Out here, his quiet confidence, his gentleness gave her assurance and strength. This was his world and he was totally familiar with it.

Colton's jaw ached. Trying to win a fair fight with Malloy, what a fool he'd been. It'd just made him look bad. Yet, Annette had seemed quite sympathetic when she had treated his bruises. Colton's mind churned with anger. He'd show Malloy. No one was going to make a fool of him. But they needed Malloy. Even Colton admitted this. He'd done some camping in northern California; but this land was nothing like back home. Thinking of home, his mind drifted. He tried to remember what his father looked like, but couldn't. He vaguely remembered a tall, red-haired man. It had been so long ago. His mother had described it has a whirlwind romance. She had met Henry's father through an uncle while attending a banquet. He was an adventurous, handsome successful man. Then, Henry remembered his mother crying, pleading with his father not to go; but his father was a stubborn man. He'd had a small stake and a few investments but it wasn't enough. He was determined to have a fortune of his own to match his wife's. Well, Henry had suffered, growing up in a house of females. His father would pay for that when he found him. Then he'd show everyone-including Annette. Henry looked up.

"Annette, look!" shouted Henry.

Annette turned. A deer stood drinking from the riverbed. It looked up, at the sound of Henry's voice, then turned and crashed into the bush.

"Nice goin'," said Malloy, "that could've been dinner."
Henry glared at Malloy.

They ate lunch in the boat, Malloy relentless in pushing on. "We'll stop in an hour or two, when the sun's at its peak."

At two-thirty they made camp on a rocky shore. Malloy gassed the engine from a metal container. They were getting low on fuel. He hoped they'd make the Flat River, where there were cabins with supplies he could borrow. Colton collected firewood. It seemed to be his job. Mary prepared tea and biscuits.

As they sat around drinking tea, Malloy said, "We'll have a decision to make pretty soon. Up ahead the river branches off into Flat River, and shortly thereafter the Caribou River and Irvine Creek. If we stay on the Nahanni, we'll have to portage around Victoria Falls. Now, there's been a fair bit of prospectin' on the Flat River, and that could be where your father and brother went Miss Bouchard. On the other hand, they may have gone past the falls. We've found no evidence about what they did yet, and I don't suspect we will. What do you want to do?"

"Let's go up the Flat River. Maybe one of the prospectors remembers them," said Annette.

"That's if we find any. Most are gone, though Albert Faille might be around. He runs his trap lines then spends time searching for that valley of gold as the legend speaks of."

"Then the decision seems to be made," said Colton.

"Maybe." Malloy reached into his pocket for his pipe. "The fact is that north of Victoria Falls is a whole wilderness that's virtually unexplored. According to rumors, there's a valley near the Yukon boundary that's loaded with gold. It was this legend that the McLeod boys went after. Problem is, that there's lots of valleys within these maze of canyons. Anybody prospectin' on the Flat River has only found traces of gold. It's around fifty-three miles from the Flat River to the South Nahanni above Victoria Falls. We might start there and head north into the backcountry. Fact is it's like lookin' for a needle in a haystack."

"Well, we have to start somewhere, and if there was a lot of prospecting on the Flat River that's where we should begin," said Annette.

"You're the boss. We should reach Caribou tomorrow," said Malloy, taking a puff on his pipe.

That night they camped at near mouth of Mary's River, named after Poole Field's wife's cousin. They were only a few miles from the junction between the Nahanni and Flat River. Malloy would've preferred to push on, but Colton was beat and his neck sore with welts from mosquito bites. Annette, trouper she was, also was fatigued. Greenhorns, thought Malloy, but they were toughening. He'd also noticed changes in himself. He hadn't touched a drop from the metal flask in his pack in days. His pants were loose. He breathed deeply and felt the strength and power within him. He was lean and hard again. If only Rose could see him now. It was the first time he'd thought of her in two weeks. His mind had been pre-occupied with another woman--Annette. Malloy had to admit that he was growing fond of her. He found himself watching her often. Malloy saw how the sun highlighted her hair. Her skin once pale was now tanned. Her figure had lost some of its roundness, but none of its beauty. He reprimanded himself for looking upon her as he did. But he admitted that he was human and not all his thoughts were pure.

The storm that swept into their camp that night seemed to hold the wrath of God, but Malloy was certain it wasn't punishment for anything he'd done. Yet, Malloy admitted as his makeshift tent blew away, it certainly was a taste of hell.

CHAPTER FIVE: TEMPEST FROM HELL

Malloy shook Colton. "Wake up!"
"What is it?" croaked Colton, rubbing his eyes. Now awake, he noticed the shaking tent and whistling wind.
"Help me pull the boat ashore. There's a hell of a storm that's hit us. If anything happens to the boat we're gonna be stranded for a few days."
Colton whipped aside his blankets and pulled on his pants and boots.
"Hurry up!"
Outside the wind howled like baying wolves. Black storm clouds juggernauted above them like an oncoming army. Bursting bombs of lightning exploded in hellish displays. Cold rain lashed their faces. Malloy ran to the boat. Luckily he'd tied it down, not Colton. White-capped waves pounded the rocky shore. Malloy waded out. The current pulled at him, he staggered but maintained his balance. Colton grabbed the bow and struggled to lift it.
"Careful, don't scrape the bottom." warned Malloy.
"I'm doing my best," shouted Colton.
Struggling, they half-carried, half-dragged the boat onto the shore under the shelter of a few bushes. Malloy gathered up his gear and headed for Colton's tent.
They were both soaked. Colton was shivering.
"Best strip down and cover yourself with dry blankets. An' let's hope your tent don't blow down," said Malloy. He pulled the flask from his pack. He offered it to Colton. "This'll warm you up."
Colton took a swig. He coughed. "What is this stuff?"
"Homemade brew. It'll put hair on your chest."
"Or burn it off." Colton choked and returned the flask to Malloy, whom he noticed didn't drink but returned the flask to his pack.
"Thanks. You did all right," said Malloy.
"I try," said Colton. What about tomorrow?"
"We'll push on. Use the tent canvas as a shelter on the boat. Just have to be real careful for driftwood or logs. "
"Why not stay here?" asked Colton.
"There's lightning. We're safer in the open then we are surrounded by trees. Also the river'll rise. We'll be flooded out here. As soon as we're dried off, we'd better wake Annette and start packing. Once we get a bit of light, we'd best be off."
If it weren't for Colton's pocket watch, no one would've known when day began. The sky was still pitch black and the storm increased its fury. The river had risen several feet and the boat was now floating

on the water, near the bushes it was sheltered in. They broke camp quickly, and despite the slickers they wore, were drenched. That day they struggled upstream. Armies of waves rocked the boat. Pieces of flotsam and driftwood swept past in the churning water. Colton sat at the bow looking out for debris. Annette paddled and Malloy furiously worked the kicker in the stern. Malloy's goal was the mouth of the Flat River twelve miles away. He knew they'd probably find shelter in a nearby trapper's cache.

"Keep your eye peeled for the junction. It'll be to the left," yelled Malloy. Navigating was difficult. Dark clouds suppressed daylight. Occasional lightning burst like flares in the sky. Malloy got his visual bearings from that. In the bow Colton had a kerosene lantern and a compass.

"Log ahead!" bellowed Colton. "Go left."

Malloy heard a scrapping on the right side of the boat. Shit! Not enough room. He hoped there was no damage. The towering canyon walls and thick forest along the shores loomed over them like troops of menacing giants. Wind tore at Malloy's clothes. Rain blinded his eyes. He pulled his hat brim down.

It was taking all of Malloy's skill to keep the boat from capsizing.

"Tell Henry to keep an eye out for the channel!" yelled Malloy to Annette.

Lightning cracked. They heard a roar from above.

"Lookout!" screamed Colton.

Malloy looked up to see a huge burning tree crash down from the cliff above them on their left. Malloy jammed up the kicker and pushed the rudder trying to maneuver them out of range. He looked up and knew he wasn't going to make it. The huge tree was hurling upon them. Annette screamed!

"Jump!" yelled Malloy, as he reached forward and grabbed Annette. Together the two of them leaped into the battling waters as the flaming wood bomb smashed the boat.

CHAPTER SIX: SURVIVAL!

Malloy and Annette's heads broke the surface. They sputtered and gasped for breath. "Colton!" cried Malloy. A wave swept over him. Malloy spit water.

More lightning exploded overhead. Malloy thought he saw Colton clinging to part of the boat. He tried to swim towards him; but the current was too strong. It whirled and whipped him and Annette down stream. Malloy grabbed Annette's shirt and headed for shore.

Annette weighed him down. "If you're hangin' onto anything, let go! "He yelled.

"I've got one of the packs," she gasped.

"The weight's pullin' us under. Let go." yelled Malloy as a wave hit him. He felt his load lighten and they shot up through the raging waters. He swam towards the shore.

Time seemed to stand still. Malloy's arms felt like iron weights. It was like trying to climb up a slippery slope. He choked and spit water. Muscles burned. He was tiring; but he couldn't give up. Annette was kicking her legs, and paddling with one arm while clinging to Malloy with the other. Malloy panicked. Cold fear contracted him. He wasn't strong enough to last out. He felt his body being sucked downward. He kicked. And then, Malloy's boot scraped bottom. Land, sweet land. He struggled further, half swimming, half walking on the stony bottom until he could feel the hard bottom solid beneath his feet. He stood up. The water was above his waist. He pulled Annette up. Together, they stumbled onto the shore and collapsed. Cold wind poured over them, chilling them to the bone. Annette shivered and smiled at Malloy. In her hand was his rifle. Malloy shook his head; he rolled onto his back and laughed gratefully as the freezing rain washed the sand and mud from his sodden form. Armed, he could hunt and trap. They wouldn't starve. He crawled up into a standing position and pulled Annette to her feet.

He took the small axe from the sheath on his belt and cut several long branches from a fallen tree several yards down the shore. He dragged them into the nearby woods. Under the shelter of the spruce and pine forest he jammed two Y-shaped branches into the soft ground for lean-to supports.

"Find some pine or spruce branches, "said Malloy handing Annette his axe. Annette nodded and began searching nearby.

Despite the chilling cold they worked until the shelter was completed. The thick branches kept the rain off them. Other branches were used as bedding.

Malloy began to undress and wring out his clothes.

"No room for modesty." he said, "You'd best do the same, or you run the risk of hypothermia."

Annette stood up and began to unbutton her shirt. Malloy spread the wrung clothing over the flooring of pine branches. Annette handed Malloy her underpants. Malloy's hand reached out and froze as his eyes moved down her body. Her nakedness aroused him, and he couldn't control it. Her dark nipples jutted out from small but well-rounded breasts. Annette smiled coyly and moved closer. Malloy took her in his arms. His lips crushed hers as they kissed. They hugged each other close and sank down onto the bed of pine and spruce branches.

Later as they huddled in each other's arms, Malloy looked out at the stormy river. Thunder cannoned across the sky. The wind shrieked like screech owls. He felt her warmth and held her close. A stabbing of guilt pierced him. He was at fault. He cursed himself for not waiting. At the risk of losing the boat, they could've moved to higher ground. Malloy wondered if Henry Colton had survived.

***

Henry Colton clung onto a boulder and let the remaining bow of the boat that had been his life raft, shoot out into the churning water. He choked and coughed. During the flashes of lightning he saw other rocks nearby protruding from the river like broken teeth. Slowly he began swimming his way from rock to rock. Razor edges cut his hand. Colton struggled towards shore, his left fist clenching one of the backpacks. It pulled him down but he wasn't about to give it up. Finally he felt solid ground underfoot and clambered onto a sandy strip of beach. He saw trees several yards away, stumbled towards them and collapsed, the numbing cold giving way to inner warmth.

He shivered and awoke. Rain pelted him. Groggily he picked himself up. Pulling some rope from the pack he cut off a piece, and tied it between two trees. He peeled off his raincoat and threw it over the rope and anchored the coat down with some heavy stones. Colton crawled inside, dragging the pack behind him. Sheltered from the rain, Henry wiggled out of his clothes. He used a folding knife in the pack to stab and peeled back a tin of beans, and ate them cold. He then took stock of his supplies and discovered that he wasn't in bad shape. He'd grabbed Malloy's pack. There were three boxes of cartridges, some tins of meat, beans, and fruit, rope, and wrapped in oilcloth, extra set of clothes, including an old Stetson. He also found matches in a waterproof tin, fishing line, a small sewing kit, and a blanket.

Henry dressed in Malloy's clothes. They were too big for him, but they were relatively dry. He then did his best to wring the water out of the blanket. It was still quite damp, but he huddled into it. Fatigue overtook him and he drifted off to sleep.

Malloy found himself in a grassy sea of blood. All around him were half buried arms and legs thrusting out of the field. Hands clutched at him. He batted them away. Tommy! He cried out, but no sound burst from his mouth. Malloy felt the cold clammy hand of fear clutching him. He had to find Tommy Birk. He ran. His feet sunk into the mire, slowing him down. "NO MALLOY!" a voice cried out to him. Malloy stared into the cold morning mist seeing nothing but shadowy gray forms lying about him.

The tone of the voice was urgent, yet it seemed so distant. He heard his name again. His arms and legs felt heavy like lead. No, I must go he said. But something urged him to turn back. Go towards the voice said his mind. He fought his way up from the darkness. It was like swimming in quicksand. His eyes fluttered and opened. Lightning flashed and he saw Annette looking over him with wide eyes.

"Are you all right? You were screaming. It scared me," she said.

Malloy sat up and looked around. Lightning flashed again and he saw the beach and the swollen foaming water of the river. He groaned and lay back down. His heart was beating quickly and he was bathed in sweat. Malloy shuddered. He felt Annette next to him, her body warm and alive. He saw the concern on her face. "I had a bad dream. I'm okay now." He reached out and put his arms around her. "Really."

She hugged him. Annette didn't know what demons haunted Malloy, but she was glad that he seemed all right. The thought of being totally alone and dependent on her own skills out in this wilderness terrified her. Annette stayed awake for a while, listening to the thunderous crashing of the rain. Nestling in Malloy's arms, she finally allowed herself to relax, and soon fell back to sleep.

Annette opened an eye and was momentarily blinded by the bright sunshine. She looked around. Malloy was gone. Her clothes were still slightly damp; but she dressed and stepped outside. The sky was a deep blue and she could smell the fresh grass and pine scent from the trees. She stretched, grateful to be alive. Annette heard footsteps and turned to see Malloy step out of the bush.

"Morning." he smiled. "Found some fairly dry wood, though I suspect we'll still have a bit of smoke, and I caught us breakfast." He held up his left hand. In it was a small fish.

The wood was damp and it took Malloy a number of attempts before he managed to get a fire going. Thick gray smoke issued forth, and then, finally a yellowish spark. He blew softly on it, and added some more wood shavings. Slowly the fire gained energy. He cut open the fish with his pocket knife and cleaned it, then put it on a stick and held it over the fire.

Annette and Malloy ate greedily. Afterwards they took stock of their supplies. They had Malloy's rifle, which until Malloy could clean, was useless. Malloy had his revolver, a small axe, pocket knife and some wooden matches in a waterproof container, and his flask. Annette had a comb, and a small folding hunting knife.

"Not great, but we can survive," said Malloy. "First off, we need some transportation."

"How? We've no rope to make a raft with?" asked Annette.

"Then, I guess I'd best clean the rifle and kill us a moose."

"What?" Annette looked puzzled.

Malloy smiled. "A local trapper named Albert Faille showed me how to make a canoe with moose hide. The Indians used them. I guess that's where he learned about it."

This was easier said than done. Malloy spent the morning cleaning and checking his rifle. The rest of the day was spent tramping through the bush in search of a moose. It was to no avail. The only thing Malloy and Annette seemed to catch were insect bites. Dejected, they returned to camp late in the afternoon.

Malloy caught another fish and they ate supper. "Tomorrow, we'll start hiking. Maybe we'll find some of our supplies, hopefully some rope and I can make a raft."

"Uh-huh." mumbled Annette. She lay next to him, her head resting on his shoulder.

Malloy kissed her forehead. She looked up into his eyes. Malloy felt himself getting aroused. They kissed again. His arms drew her to him and she began unbuttoning his shirt.

Henry Colton ate hot beans that he'd cooked in the tin. He had a warm fire going. He'd spent the day combing the beach trying to find more supplies. Another pack had washed up on shore. It was Annette's. He wondered if she were alive. He took it back to camp.

Colton knew he couldn't stay here forever. His supplies would run out soon. Tomorrow he'd have to head out. He laid back, his head resting on a log and stared up at the sky. He breathed deeply and relaxed. He felt his eyes grow heavy when he heard a soft rustling coming from the bush.

Colton bolted up and listened. It didn't sound like human footsteps. He looked around. The fire may keep it or them away. But he needed a weapon. If he could kill the animal, he'd have fresh meat. He looked around and found two sharp rocks. He clutched both of them, turned towards where he'd heard the sounds. He stood still, staring into the black forest. Another rustling sound. He saw two glowing eyes in the bush. A moment later a large gray wolf stepped out, followed by three others.

"Oh shit," muttered Colton. He glanced at the tree by his tent. He wondered how high wolves could jump.

The leader of the pack growled and stepped towards Colton. Colton's stomach tightened and sweat broke out on his brow. They must've smelled the food. The wolf lowered his haunches, ready to charge.

Colton prayed his aim was true. His fist tightened around the rock in his right hand and he hurled it at the lead wolf.

Malloy and Annette had finished making love and were nestled in each other's arms. Suddenly a human cry a blood-curdling scream pierced the stillness and echoed across the river valley. Malloy sat up. He looked at Annette.

"Henry?" whispered Annette.

CHAPTER SEVEN: REUNITED

There wasn't anything Malloy could do at night. But he knew that the next morning he'd have to find some way for them to cross the river.

"Hell or high water, we move out tomorrow," he said. "Now we'd best get some sleep. We're gonna have a long day tomorrow."

Annette slept fitfully that night, worried about Colton and unsure of her blossoming relationship with Malloy. It was dawn when she awoke. Annette yawned, then gasped. A bull moose and a cow were drinking at the river. She shook Malloy.

Malloy stretched and looked towards Annette's pointed finger. He blinked, smiled and reached for his rifle. He rolled onto his stomach and aimed. The Enfield roared in the early morning silence. Birds scattered. The moose went down. Malloy fired again.

"Someone up there's watching over us. Maybe food will smoke him out for us, because we're gonna have us a fine breakfast. We'd better get to it," he said while pulling his axe from its sheath.

Annette dressed and started the fire while Malloy began skinning and butchering the two moose. Within minutes he looked like a barbarian warrior after a battle. His long johns were soon covered in blood. He handed Annette two chunks of meat. Making a spit, Annette cooked some steaks.

After they ate, Malloy made a wooden frame and dried the skins. "These hides are going to have to dry." He then started salvaging all useable parts.

After he finished Malloy bathed in the river and spent the rest of the day salvaging the forest for some usable spruce branches. These he trimmed and cut into usable pieces for the frame.

That evening with Annette cradled in his arms, they sat and watched the sunset. The sky turned to crimson and the snow-capped mountains glowed like they were on fire. Later in the comfort of their lean-to, Malloy undressed Annette and gently explored her body. His craving for Annette grew. She pulled him to her. They kissed, their lips crushing each other. They made love.

The next morning and a good part of the afternoon were used making the canoe. Malloy made a frame of spruce poles and tied them with babiche(dried rawhide). Using sinew, and a needle made from bone, Malloy sewed the hides together and stretched them over the frame. Malloy used more babiche to tie the hides along the gunwales.

Next he flattened and forced small pieces of peeled spruce between the hide and the frame to serve as ribs. Then, Malloy fashioned a couple of oars.

"Will it float?" asked Annette.

"Yeah, but they sit low in the water and are fragile. We'll have to be really careful and watch out for rocks and logs." Malloy looked up at the sky. "It's getting late in the afternoon. We'd best be off."

Annette packed up their supplies and some extra meat. They loaded the canoe and shoved off. Malloy sat in the stern and Annette in the bow.

Henry David Colton was cold, hungry and afraid. His hands were numb from clinging to the tree trunk; his right leg ached where the wolf had bit him, but at least it had stopped bleeding. He had used one of his shirtsleeves as a tourniquet and bandage. Henry looked down from the branch where he sat. The remaining wolf was pacing and growling below. Colton had killed the leader. The rocks had hit the wolf in the head, stunning him. Henry snatched a flaming log from the fire and thrust it at the wolf, setting it on fire. It yelped in agony and twisted away. He turned and swung the firebrand to ward off the other two wolves. Slowly, Henry inched away towards a spruce tree with low branches; but one of the wolves sneaked around from behind and bit him.

Colton thrust the flaming log into the wolf's face. It yelped and rolled on the ground and into the fire where flames engulfed it. The third wolf ran off. Wounded and tired, Colton managed to climb up a tree. The third wolf returned and leaped at him, but couldn't reach him. It now waited below. The other two carcasses lay smouldering. To show his contempt, Colton urinated on the wolf as it paced below. This irritated the animal, and brought some satisfaction to Colton.

"Go left, log coming up," cautioned Annette.

Malloy saw it and steered around it. He kept his eyes peeled along the shore, looking for Colton. Malloy reasoned that if Colton had survived, he'd camp along the shore.

Colton looked out. He saw a canoe with two people aboard mid-river. He began to yell.

"HELP! OVER HERE! HELP!"

They'd been travelling about an hour. Annette turned to Malloy. "I hear someone shouting."

"So do I. Over there." Malloy pointed. He began paddling towards the shore.

"Do you think its Henry?" asked Annette.

"Won't know til we get there, but it sure sounds like him. I hear him, but I can't see him," said Malloy.

"Neither can I."

Malloy squinted." I think I see a yellow tent in the bush."

They could both here a man shouting clearly now. "Malloy, help! Over here!"

As they neared shore, Malloy and Annette jumped out.

"Lift the canoe. We can't afford ripping the bottom out."

The wolf heard the approach of other humans. It sniffed the air and ran into the bush.

"Annette!" cried Henry.

"Henry? Where are you?" called Annette.

"Up here."

Malloy and Annette looked up. A bedraggled Henry Colton was perched on a thick branch about twelve feet up. Then Malloy saw the two carcasses. Another wolf.

"It treed me," explained Colton as he climbed down.

Malloy heard a rustle in the bush. He turned and fired. A yelp and thrashing followed. "He won't bother you now."

Malloy examined the camp. "Looks like you did quite well." He checked the supplies in the packs. "Well, at least we have some supplies."

He turned and stifled a laugh. Colton was wearing his spare shirt and pants. The pants were bunched up at the waist. A piece of rope was used as a belt. The legs were rolled up with thick cuffs. The shirt hung on Colton like he was a scarecrow.

"My clothes were wet," said Colton.

"Did I say anything?" Malloy tried to look innocent.

"You're hurt." said Annette. "Let me look at it."

"Wolf bit me on the calf." explained Colton. He winced as she untied the dirty piece of material.

"Is there any first aid kit?" she asked.

"No."

"Let me have a look. "Malloy bent over." Not too bad at least you won't need stitches, but he broke the skin. Best wash it out with this." Malloy pulled out his flask from his belt. "This'll kill any germs. Then re-bandage it."

He left Annette and Colton to find some firewood. Malloy thought about Annette. He wondered what she would say to Colton. Would she tell him about her and Malloy's lovemaking? Malloy hoped that Annette wouldn't say anything until they got out of all this mess. It was going to take all of them to survive.

The canoe wouldn't be strong enough to hold all three of them. Malloy would have to make a raft. He knew they were getting close to Virginia Falls. Malloy would have to backtrack to go down the

Caribou River. There were a lot of trappers who kept caches and cabins along there. When they found one, they could replenish their supplies. Out in the northwest, everyone depended upon everyone else. Cabins and supplies were shared. You paid the person back when you could. Malloy returned to camp with an armful of firewood. Colton was resting in his makeshift tent. Annette had changed clothes. She wore a red checked shirt and blue serge trousers tucked into her boots. Her hair was combed and a tied back with a red ribbon. The supplies were laid out neatly by the two packs. "I'm taking inventory. I don't think we're bad off."

Malloy smiled and began making a fire. "You find a pot so I can make some tea?"

"As a matter of fact I have. It was half buried in some muck on the shore," she replied.

"You look great Annie," Malloy smiled.

Annette threw a glance towards the tent. "Please," she whispered.

Colton woke an hour later. Over a lunch of tea and moose steaks, they made plans.

"The fact is that until we get some new supplies and build another boat, we're in no shape to continue the search for your father," said Malloy," Now what I propose is that we go back and head down the Flat River. There's a lot of caches and cabins there. We can borrow some supplies. From there we can head either west or north on foot."

"Personally, I think we should just go back. We have no idea where they are," complained Colton. "I've had enough of the great outdoors."

"Coward!" spat Annette. "We've come this far. Maybe we'll meet someone who remembers them."

"Finding people here is like looking for a needle in a haystack darling," snapped Colton. He gestured, throwing his arms wide. "For god sakes look at us Annette. We've barely survived these past three weeks. The likelihood of your father and Andre surviving for two years out here is preposterous." Colton stood up and finished his coffee. "I'm no quitter, but this is not my world out here. I'm tired, and bitten alive. You've got to be realistic about these things."

Annette glared at Henry. She looked at Malloy. He remained silent for the moment; letting Colton, continue his tirade.

"Annette, if I could've hired a plane we could've combed the area much faster. If they left any kind of sign, we'd probably be able to spot it from the air. But on the ground? It'll take us..." Colton left the sentence unfinished. He looked towards Malloy for support.

Malloy nodded towards Annie. "Annie knows the risks Colton. Besides, we will probably find something down on the Flat. There's still a few prospectors poking about. We've got a few more weeks, and then we'll have to head back. We can't afford to get trapped here for the winter."

"Annie? You called Annette..." Colton's voice dropped.

"It's shorter and friendlier than Annette. Don't get your dander up," said Malloy.

"Yeah." Colton looked at Annette and Malloy. The seed of suspicion began to grow. They'd been by themselves for almost three days. Did anything happen between them? A jealous rage began to seep into Colton's mind. He would watch them. And as soon as Malloy's usefulness was through, he'd kill the old geezer.

CHAPTER EIGHT: ON THE FLAT RIVER

July, 1937

The embers in the fire grew low. They turned in. Annette slept in her own lean-to, and Colton and Malloy shared a larger makeshift tent. The next morning was bright and hot. Flies buzzed viciously around the campsite. Malloy and Colton, taking turns began cutting down trees for the raft. Together they dragged the logs down to the beach where Malloy split them. Later he would lash them together with rope. It was hard work. Despite the mosquitoes and dreaded black flies, both men stripped off their shirts. Sweat glistened on their tanned torsos.

Annette watched them as she packed up the camp. Malloy's body was lean and hard. She'd also noticed that Colton's soft body was starting to develop a more muscular look. It aroused her.

Malloy took a couple of long planks and fashioned paddles and a crude rudder. By late afternoon they were ready to leave.

"Let's go. We've got a few hours of daylight, we might as well use them," said Malloy.

It took all three of them to launch the raft. The moose hide canoe was tied to one side. The water was cool and refreshing. They ate a cold supper as they paddled down the river. It took them forty-five minutes to reach the Flat River. An hour later Malloy pointed towards wooded shore. A log cabin with a thatched roof was visible near the shore.

They beached the raft and tied it down. "Stay here." ordered Malloy. He knocked on the door. "Anyone home?" he called out. "Looks like it belongs to Albert Faille, a trapper-prospector I know. We call him Red pants because of the red flannel trousers he always wears. We can replenish our supplies. I'll leave Albert a note and pay him back when we get back to town. We'll make camp here. Annie can sleep in the cabin, we'll camp outside Colton."

"Sounds fine. I'm bushed."

The next day they continued down the Flat River. They were in a flat grassy valley. The mountains were a deep blue mass in the distance. The air was fresh and alive with the sounds of birds and insect life.

"Shades of Huckleberry Finn," commented Colton as they drifted down the river.

"Keep your eyes peeled for signs of placer mining. As I said, there should be a few fellows prospecting along here. We'll question anyone we see. Do you still have those pictures Annie?"

"Yes." said Annette. She lay on the raft; her head propped up on a pack and stared at the blue sky and white clouds. She felt the sun warm her and suddenly she wished she had a bathing suit. An impish smile crossed her lips. Annette stood up and began to unbutton her blouse.

"What in the hell do you think you're doing?" cried Colton.

"Getting some sun. There's no one around."

Colton glanced at Malloy who'd been looking along the shore until the conversation started. Malloy grinned as he watched Annette undress.

"The least you could do is turn your head," snapped Colton. "Annette my darling..."

Annette dropped her shirt. She sat down and pulled off her boots and socks, then stood up and unbuckled her pants. She wore a camisole and underpants underneath. Using her pants and shirt as a towel, she lay back down.

" ...What the hell has gotten into you?" finished Colton. He stared at her. Their courtship had been quite reserved. His eyes trailed down her trim legs. He saw her erect nipples outlined through the thin material. Colton knew he wanted her. Just as he knew he would kill Malloy.

It was a couple of hours later they reached a branch in the river. Malloy steered the raft towards shore.

"Why are we going ashore?" asked Colton.

There's something I want to show you. Better get your clothes on Annie," said Malloy.

Annette stretched and smiled. She pulled her pants on, and laced up her boots. She knew both men were watching her. She buttoned her shirt slowly, enjoying the erotic feeling it gave her.

Malloy and Colton tied the raft. "Follow me," said Malloy.

Annette and Colton followed Malloy a little ways into the bush. In a clearing were the remains of a burnt cabin. "This is where Phil Powers died," said Malloy. "A piece of paper was found near the cabin. It read: ' Phil Powers finished August, 1932.'"

A shiver went down Annette's spine. "He's one of the murdered men you told us about isn't he?"

"That's right. Just his skeleton remained. Powers' was laying half way between the cabin and the beach. The bones were bleached, as if he'd been lying there for ages, and given the cause of death, his bones should've been charred. They found twelve empty cartridges by the body, but no sign of Powers' rifle, and he'd just purchased a new Savage. The Mounties identified him by his teeth and some personal articles. That was around five years ago. Never found out what caused the fire or what exactly killed Powers. But Phil was a prospector in these parts, and now he's part of the legend."

Silence hung in the clearing like a dying bagpipe. Annette moved closer to Malloy. She wanted to hold him, but she was also conscious of Henry and didn't want to arouse any more animosity in him.

"Let's go," said Malloy.

Colton stared at the burnt ruins. His eyes shifted around. Why did he feel they were being watched? "Uh, Malloy, come here."

Malloy and Annette turned. They'd started heading back. "What is it?" asked Malloy.

Colton came close and whispered. "I think we're being watched."

Malloy grinned. "Could be. There's lots of us that have had that feeling out here. It's part of the mystery."

"I'm serious," stated Colton.

"I know you are. So am I. Let's go."

Ten minutes later they were back on the river. Both Colton and Annette felt more at ease.

"Look, a cabin," said Annette as she pointed to the shore. A small log cabin stood out in clearing near the beach.

"Prospector or trapper, they've got 'em scattered all over here." Explained Malloy. "You want to make camp? It's probably about time. We've put in a good day."

"Sounds fine to me," agreed Colton.

"Well, then that's that. We'll stop," said Malloy.

Inside the cabin was a homemade bunk, a table and chairs, trapping equipment and shelves stocked with sugar, flour, canned goods and a few cooking utensils. In a shed attached to the cabin were winter supplies: a sled, snowshoes and a heavy fur coat.

Against one wall was a drum oven. This was a small, round tin oven attached to the stovepipe. "I'm going to make some biscuits," announced Annette. "Now you two men go out for awhile and let me cook."

"Let's go Colton, we can have a look around," said Malloy.

They followed a narrow trail near the beach, skirting the wide expanse of grassland. The land was flat with tall grass and clumps of trees. The forest line was back further towards the mountain. Colton walked ahead. Suddenly he tripped. "Uh.."

Malloy saw him fall. "You all right Colton?"

"Yeah, I tripped over this wooden chute contraption."

Malloy went over. Colton was standing, brushing himself off.

"This is part of a sluice gate. It's placer mine set-up. This chute is usually attached to a hopper at the higher end. The hopper sifts dirt. What's left is larger material, hopefully gold. Usually one of these aren't' built unless the prospect is good. Normally a gold pan's used first. Somebody was sure hopeful."

"So where are the prospectors?" asked Colton.

"Well, this one's been here a while, see how the wood's weathered? Looks like somebody tried to hide it too. "Malloy uncovered more of the trough."Let's look around some more."

Both men followed the trough back and found the rocker hidden by some overgrown shrubs. "Let's look around for the campsite."

Colton and Malloy split up. Colton headed back towards the beach, while Malloy walked inland. Colton found a battered gold pan three-quarters buried beneath grit and rocks on the beach. He sat on his haunches and stared at the water. He dipped the pan into the sand and lifted it up, his fingers sifted through the material as it swirled around. Gold thought Colton.

About one hundred yards inland from the river Malloy found the skeletal remains of a campsite. An abandoned shovel, some rotted canvas and tent pegs, and an empty tin. The weather aged remnants like these quickly. Malloy looked around some more. There were lots of sites like this one dotting Irvine Creek. Who knew if one of these belonged to George and Andre Bouchard? There were a lot of greenhorns back in '31 and '32. Malloy stood up and turned to go, when he spotted something glittering in the grass. He walked over and bent down. His fingers pried the object from the packed dirt and grass. Malloy brushed off the caked dirt. It was a locket. Using some spit, he wiped it more thoroughly. It was a gold locket. Malloy opened it up. Inside were pictures of two women. One of them was Annette!

CHAPTER NINE: FACE IN THE WINDOW

"Have you ever seen this before?" asked Malloy as he and Colton entered the cabin.

Annette took a pan of biscuits out of the stove. Annette froze as she saw the locket dangling from Malloy's hand. Her hands trembled.

"It was Papa's! Where did you find it?" Annette tossed the pan down on the stovetop and dashed across the small cabin. She snatched the locket from Malloy.

"Not far from here, in fact it's pretty amazing we did find this," marvelled Malloy, "considering the size of the area. I don't think you realize the chances of finding evidence like this so soon, especially when we haven't really been looking so hard."

"Who cares, the fact is you did find it. Now what?" asked Colton.

"We could work our way inland. Evidence shows us that this is where George and Andre Bouchard worked their claim. Obviously something or someone led them away from this spot. The campsite is old. They may have moved on to new digs. Problem is that there isn't the rush there was two years ago. Very few people are here now. We'll scout around and see if we find anyone else prospecting. Maybe they'll remember them."

"What about the person who made this cabin?" asked Annette.

"I'm not sure who's this is. If it's Faille's, well we could have a long wait. Old Albert's got lots of caches up and down the river, and so do many other trappers and prospectors in the area. It's just common survival sense is all. But the fact is you could go for weeks on end before sighting anyone."

"Isn't there anything in the legends around here that would indicate which direction that valley of gold was supposed to be in?" queried Colton.

"West, towards the mountains. Problems with legends are that there's usually very little truth in them," replied Malloy.

"Well, we can make plans later. Dinner is ready," announced Annette happily. Malloy noticed that she wore the locket around her neck.

After dinner Malloy and Colton, using a large piece of canvas they'd found in the cabin, set up a tent outside. Malloy built a fire. It would supply some light and warmth, as well as be a signal to anyone passing by. Colton turned in.

Malloy sat down on a piece of driftwood and lit his pipe. He took his flask out. Funny, he hadn't had the urge in sometime. Perhaps it was the fact that he was busy again, or maybe it was Annette's influence. But tonight he wanted a drink just to relax with. He unscrewed the cap and took a swig. It burned his throat. Malloy took a puff on his pipe and put the flask away.

Annette came out. She wore one of his shirts. Her feet were bare. She crouched down next to Malloy. He glanced at her. "You'll catch cold like that."

"I'm almost ready to turn in. Is Henry asleep?" Malloy nodded and thumbed towards the tent. They could hear Henry snoring.

"Outdoors tires a person out."

Annette smiled. "I know. I don't think I've slept this well since Papa and Andre left."

Malloy patted Annette's knee. Annette placed her hand over his. Their eyes met. Malloy glanced at the tent. "Annie, you'd best get some sleep. We could have a real busy day tomorrow."

Annette leaned over and kissed Malloy on the cheek then went inside the cabin. Malloy watched her go. He felt the urge to join her, but with Colton around it'd be plain stupid. What was he getting himself into? He was old enough to be her father. He shook his head, sighed and puffed on his pipe looking up at the stars.

Suddenly he heard a scream from within the cabin.

"Annie!" he cried and bolted up.

Inside the cabin he found Annette huddled on the bed. She pointed at the window at the back of the cabin. "I saw a face peering in."

"Stay here," ordered Malloy. He went to the tent and woke Colton.

"What's up? Was that Annie crying?" mumbled Henry.

"Watch Annie."

Malloy snatched a lighted stick from the campfire and ran around to the back of the cabin. The burning stick was clutched in his left hand, while his right held his revolver. Below the window the grass was crushed. Noting more crushed grass leading away from the cabin, Malloy started his pursuit.

Clouds lifted and the moon shone bright. Malloy kept a moderate pace, checking for broken branches and crushed long grass. Malloy was almost to the tree line when he heard gunshots coming from the river. Malloy whirled around and ran back to the cabin. He heard three more gunshots. Malloy ran faster. His heart pounded. He wheezed. His long legs covered the ground quickly. Minutes ticked by like hours. Finally he sighted the cabin.

Breaking out of the brush, Malloy ran to the river. He saw a figure lying in the grass. His rifle lay nearby. Malloy bent over. It was

Colton. There was a cut on his forehead. "Annie," he gasped. "They got Annie."

CHAPTER TEN: ON THE TRAIL

"Who were they?" asked Malloy. Taking a clean rag and pouring some water over it, he placed it on Colton's cut. "Hold this here for a minute." Then he started packing up their gear.

"I couldn't see. They hit me from behind. But I heard voices. Couldn't understand what was being said, but I think I counted at least three voices," said Colton, holding the cold wet rag to his head.

"You feeling all right?"

Colton nodded and tied the rag around his head.

"We'll start after them. Normally I'd wait until daylight, but the moon's out and it's bright enough."

Fifteen minutes later they were trotting down an old deer trail, heading north and inland. Colton was panting. Sweat stung his eyes. He was feeling dizzy.

"Can we slow down?" he gasped.

Malloy stopped. His lungs were heaving too. "Sure. Smarter thing to do anyway. If one of us trips and gets injured, it'll do us in." They marched on. The low grassland gave way to thick mixed wood forest. Towering trees hid the moon. Malloy stopped.

"I think they're heading into the mountains. We'll have to wait until daylight now. I can't track them in the dark."

"How can they move so fast?" asked Colton.

"They know the way. In fact, they've probably been trailing us for some time. I'll bet they even planted the locket I found. They've wanted Annette all along," said Malloy. He sat down and rested against a spruce tree. He pulled out his pipe and tobacco.

"But why?"

"I can think of a few reasons, and none of 'em are pleasant. Best not to speculate. We'll find her. Why don't you rest. We'll be up at sunrise."

Morning light snaked its way through the forest and speckled its floor. Malloy shook Colton awake.

"Time to move out."

Colton groaned. His head felt two sizes too large. He rolled over and sat up.

"Here, have some of this, it'll give you energy," said Malloy as he shoved a stick of beef jerky into Colton's right hand.

Colton bit off a piece of jerky and chewed it slowly. He rolled up his blanket and Malloy shoved it into his pack.

There seemed to be a beaten path through the trees. Malloy and Colton followed it. Suddenly Malloy bent down and studied some bent grass near the base of a spruce tree.

"Damn!"

"What's the matter?" asked Colton.

"We've been tricked. Annette didn't come this way." Malloy stood up.

"How can you tell?"

"The tracks. We've been following a single runner. Unfortunately it was too dark to study the tracks clearly last night. I was trailing by the bent brush and broken branches. But the track I found indicates that Annette nor more than one man went by."

"Then they split up," spat Colton.

"Annette wouldn't have gone voluntarily. If she struggled, there would be signs. If they carried her, the tracks would indicate it." Malloy shook his head. "We've been decoyed. If there were three, then two of them, with Annette, double backed to the river. The other led us up here. We've got to get back to our river camp."

They'd travelled further than Malloy had originally thought; it was mid-afternoon when they reached the cabin. The air hung heavily in the sun-drenched river valley. Both men were sweating heavily, and itching from insect bites.

"We'll repack our gear, then head out in the canoe."

"How do you know which way they went?" asked Colton. He'd taken off his boots and was soaking his feet in the water.

"Most of the immediate area's been prospected pretty heavily, except west and northwest of here. If we're looking for the unknown, that's where it's likely to be. Come on; time to get a move on. The longer we wait, the further Annette gets and the less likely the chances of finding her."

Half an hour later the two men set out in the moose hide canoe. Malloy sat in the stern so that he could steer. His blue-gray eyes scanned the shore. "There's where they entered from," he pointed. "See the crushed grass."

Colton turned and glanced at the shore. "You were right. They did use the river."

They paddled in silence, each man lost in his own thoughts and blame. The sun beat down on them. Malloy reached into his pack and pulled out his Stetson. It was like the old days when he was with the force. The thrill of the chase was in him again; he knew he'd fine Annie. Malloy thought about her supple young body. He remembered their lovemaking. The memory of her deep blue eyes burned within him. And he'd done something he'd vowed not to do-- he got involved. And it felt good.

Colton swatted a fly. His arms ached. He hated it all. He thought about having a drink in the cool lounge of his club. He looked around at the forested mountains looming up from the grassy meadows. The outdoors scared him. He'd never been camping. His father had left long before he'd been old enough for such activities, and his mother was a civilized, society woman. The thought of sleeping outside in the wilderness was unthinkable. But he never told Annette about it. He couldn't. And now look at him. But it'd be worth it, in the end.

***

Annette huddled in the middle of a long wooden canoe. Her two native captors now clad only in breechcloths silently paddled down the river. She'd heard footsteps and went outside the cabin to see who it was. Two strong hands had grabbed and gagged her. Her struggles had been in vain. She'd seen Henry's still body and prayed that he hadn't been murdered. Annette's hands were tied in front of her and she'd been led into the bush a short ways, then to the shore and into a canoe. Her captors hadn't spoken at all. One man was tall and broad-shouldered, with fine muscles. The other man was shorter and huskier but very muscular as well. Both had dark skin and long black hair that was parted in the middle and braided on the sides. They'd worn deerskin leggings, tunics and moccasins.

They ate a cold breakfast of jerky, bannock, and water while still travelling. As the day had gotten warmer, they'd stripped off most of their outer clothing.

Annette knew that Malloy would follow. Somehow she had to leave a sign for him. She turned to the Indian behind her.

"I have to go to the bathroom."

He stared at her. His face showed no expression. Oh great, thought Annette, he doesn't understand English. She looked into his dark eyes and repeated herself in French.

The native gasped. "You speak the Queen's tongue!"

The other native at the bow turned. "What is it?"

"The woman speaks our mother's tongue."

"What does she want?" asked the tall native.

"She must relieve herself."

The tall native looked at Annette in disgust. Annette then noticed that he had green-eyes.

"Head for shore." said Green-eyes to his partner, and to Annette he said, "Do not try to escape."

"Where would I go? I don't know this land," she replied.

They landed on a grassy bank. Green-eyes indicated some bushes nearby. "Hurry."

Annette ran into the bushes and crouched down. She pulled out her shirt and tore a small corner off, then reached across and tied it on a branch opposite from view of her captors. She hoped Malloy would see the red plaid signal. She tucked her shirt in, then stood up and returned to her captors.

The shorter native helped her into the canoe and they shoved off.

They travelled for hours without stopping. The mountains grew closer and the riverbanks grew higher until steep cliffs towered on either side of the canoe.

"How much further are you taking me?" asked Annette.

The natives ignored her and continued to paddle. Annette stared into the dark water and debated about diving in and taking her chances swimming. The taller native watched her and seemed to divine her thoughts. "You do not want to try to escape. The water currents are powerful and will pull you under. You will drown."

Annette sighed. She had to think of someway to leave another sign for Malloy and Henry to follow.

***

Malloy and Colton were paddled steadily up river. They had reached the area where Annette and her captives had first stopped.

"Head towards shore," said Malloy.

"You see something?"

"Looks like someone may have camped or stopped here. See the torn grass and mud higher up on the bank? Like someone dragged a canoe or boat?"

"No," said Colton. He studied the riverbank, but could not see the clues Malloy pointed out. He jumped out and pulled the canoe in. He tied the end of a rope to a small bush near the bank. "Wait here."

Malloy walked up the bank towards some bushes. A few minutes later he returned holding what looked like a piece of plaid cloth. "It's from Annette's shirt. I found it in some bushes. She's alive and they came this way."

"Well, what are we waiting for?" snapped Colton. "Let's go."

Sunlight still brightened the early evening sky. Colton's arms were numb. He turned his head and watched Malloy. Didn't the man ever tire? Despite Malloy's age, he was in far better condition than Colton had suspected. During their travels the years seemed to peel off Malloy, and Colton glimpsed the image of the man's youth.

Grudgingly, Colton began to admire and respect Malloy. He was definitely a man to be reckoned with.

"Tired?" asked Malloy.

Colton shrugged.

"It's been a long day. We'll camp soon," said Malloy. "You see anything?"

"Nope, just lots of grass, forest and mountains," replied Colton.

An hour later Malloy and Colton landed on a small stretch of pebbly beach. Colton erected the tent and gathered firewood while Malloy tried his hand at finding some small game. Unfortunately that proved futile and the two men supped on hot tea, biscuits and two tins of canned corned beef.

"A man could get lost pretty easily out here," commented Colton as he looked up at the dusky sky.

"That's what I told you."

"How long are we going to stay on the river?"

"We'll keep going until we find some sign that they left it. This river is heading north now."

***

"How much further do we have to go?" asked Annette.

Green -eyes looked up from his plate of stew. "Tomorrow if all goes well, you meet Mother Queen. Eat, and then sleep. Long day tomorrow. Perhaps you will not be as ill. Feel better."

Annette finished her stew. The other Indian had made it from some vegetables and fish. It was mildly spicy. She ate it all. Annette thought about Malloy and Henry. Had they found her signs? Were they near? She looked up at the stars and shivered. This was all like some jungle film she'd seen in the cinema. But it was real. Annette had learned very little from her captors. They were not inclined to talk. She found the silence unsettling.

Annette curled up in a furred hide that they had given her. Sleep was overcoming her when she heard a twig snap. She laid still and peeked though half-opened eyes. Both her captors leaped to their feet, knives drawn. Another Indian came out of the woods. It was the third one. He was tall and broad shouldered with a hawk like face. He greeted his friends. Then he spoke seriously at length in some Indian tongue that Annette couldn't comprehend. When he was finished, he and the shorter Indian disappeared into the bush.

***

Malloy awoke suddenly. He lay still and stared out at the darkness. He strained his ears. Footsteps. Moccasins. Whispers. They were very close. He reached for his Colt, which lay next to him. He cocked the hammer. Malloy took aim at the tent opening. A head peeked in. A hand holding the tent open also held a razor sharp curved axe. It glittered in the moonlight. Malloy fired point blank.

The roar dissolved into a flash and a scream. Colton bolted upright.

"What the hell---"

Malloy was up and rushing out of the tent. A body lay in his path. He jumped over it. He saw another figure run towards the water.

"Halt!"

The figure kept running. Malloy saw the canoe at the water's edge. Malloy fired twice. His first shot whizzed over the mystery figure's head. The second hit the man's canoe. The figure stopped and turned. He held a silvery disk in his hand.

"Drop the--," ordered Malloy. He saw the man's hand flick and the silvery whizzed towards him. Malloy dropped to the ground, the spinning disk shot over his head and landed with a thunk into a tree trunk. He fired his revolver at the figure and shouted at the man in French, then in one of the local Native dialects.

The man froze. Malloy jogged to him. The man was an Indian, tall, strong looking. Malloy kept his eyes and gun on the man as he reached over and snatched the sheafed knife from the man's side. The Indian's eyes followed Malloy's movements. "Don't even think about it," said Malloy.

"What's going on?" Colton hopped up, buttoning his pants and trying to carry a rifle all at the same time. "There's a dead savage outside the tent." He looked up and gawked at the imposing figure Malloy was covering.

"A couple of bushwhackers," replied Malloy. He glanced over and saw the rifle. "Keep an eye on this one while I get some rope. Then we're gonna ask him some questions."

"About Annie?"

"Among other things." Malloy started towards the tent, "If he tries anything, shoot him."

Malloy stepped over the prone figure outside the tent. His bullet had blown part of the Indian's face away. Inside, he rummaged in his pack for some extra rope.

Colton yelled. Malloy rushed out of the tent. He saw Colton on his knees. The Indian was struggling to take the rifle from Colton's clutched hands. The native kicked Colton in the head. Colton's grip loosened and the native tugged the rifle free.

Malloy raised his revolver and fired. He hit the Indian in the right shoulder. The native spun around and staggered. Malloy was on him. He swung his right fist down and slammed the gun barrel onto the Indian's head. The native collapsed. Malloy went over to Colton.

"You all right."

Colton grimaced and rubbed his head. "Yeah, he suckered me. You kill him?"

"No, but he'll bleed to death if I don't patch him up. Come on, give me a hand."

CHAPTER ELEVEN: PRISONERS

The sun was just spreading its soft fingers across the sheet of night sky when Annette was shaken awake. "What is it?"

"We go. Dress. Eat," said Green-eyes.

The cold morning air nipped her face. Annette shivered and stretched. Bravely she threw off the deerskin hide her captives had given her as a blanket. The ground was wet with dew. She slowly walked towards the bush.

"Don't go far," warned Green-eyes. He sat on his haunches feeding the fire and boiling water. His eyes followed her.

"Where are the others?" asked Annette. She'd found a fairly thick group of bushes behind which she could relieve herself.

"You not worry. Hurry up."

But Annette did worry. She thought she'd heard a gunshot earlier, and two of her captors were missing. Annette assumed that they had been sent back to attack Malloy and Henry. Having heard the gunshot, she surmised that Malloy and Henry were not far behind. This hope gave her strength and renewed her determination not to be afraid.

"Have tea. We leave quick," said Green-eyes.

Annette came out of the bushes and sat down on a log near the fire. The native handed her a wooden cup. Annette drank the steaming liquid. "Don't we get anything to eat? I'm hungry."

"We eat later. No time now.Hurry."

The Indian seemed restless and aggressive. Annette obeyed. She didn't want to anger him. Things weren't going as planned. And that suited Annette just fine.

Green-eyes packed up their meager camp as she finished her tea. He loaded their supplies into the canoe. Annette barely finished her tea, when the Indian hustled her aboard and shoved off. He paddled swiftly. Soon their campsite was out of view.

***

Malloy finished binding the native's wound. Their captive was securely tied and sitting against a spruce tree. He stood over the native, holding the silvery metal disk. "Interesting weapon here, this edge is razor sharp. It would've taken my head clean off." The native stared coldly at Malloy.

"He's a tough one," said Colton.

"We'll see. Okay friend, where's your partners and what have you done with Annette?" asked Malloy.

The native continued to stare blankly at Malloy. Malloy repeated himself in one of the local native dialects. A flicker of recognition passed across the Indian's eyes, but he remained silent.

"Talkative fellow isn't he," said Colton.

"Oh, he understood me, but he's the brave silent type." Malloy looked away from the Indian and towards the river. "They can't be that far ahead of us. We'll pack up and travel on down. We should be able to find their campsite. "Malloy glanced at the prisoner. The Indian's expression of interest his conversation with Colton passed quickly. Malloy smiled inwardly. So the fellow did understand English.

"We take him with us?" asked Colton, thumbing towards their prisoner.

"Yes, we've no choice."

"I'll get a shovel." Colton started to walk toward the tent.

"What for?"

Colton stopped. He turned and looked curiously at Malloy.

"To bury his friend."

"There isn't time. Besides, they place the body up in a tree. Burying him would be an insult."

Malloy and Colton hastily broke came and piled their supplies and prisoner into the canoe. Malloy watched their captive carefully as the shoved off. But the native made no attempt to jump overboard or upset the canoe. With a stoic expression he remained seated. Colton's coordination at paddling had greatly improved, and the men struck a steady rhythmic pace. It was twenty minutes later when Malloy spotted the broken brush and canoe tracks leading towards the river. "That's where they were camped." He pointed towards the area.

"Are we going to stop and investigate?" asked Colton.

"Why bother? They've gone. At least we know we're heading in the right direction."

"Yeah, but to where?"

And that question was on Malloy's mind too. He didn't know of any native tribes living in this area. In fact, the locals, because of superstition, rarely ventured this far up river. Very little was known about the area and the only one who might was old Redpants. But it was a bit too late to ask Albert now. Malloy looked up and saw that the riverbanks were starting to gather height though he doubted the walls were as high as the first or second canyon.

***

Ahead, Annette's captor landed the canoe.

"Where are we going?" Annette asked.

"Quiet woman, "ordered Green-eyes, as he helped Annette out of the canoe. He then pulled the canoe ashore and hid it in some bushes. "Come." He took her arm and headed into the forested slopes. Mosquitoes and small black flies dive-bombed mercilessly around them. Annette swatted them away. Her captor urged her on. They hiked for what seemed like hours. The trail was almost non-existent in places, overgrown with brush; but it was still visible, like a narrow deer trail. They climbed upwards. The thick forest of pine and spruce obliterated the sunlight.

"Can't we rest?" asked Annette," I'm tired, and thirsty."

"We rest soon. Hurry." Green-eyes, gave her a light shove.

Annette's legs ached. She left dizzy. "I have to rest."

They had broken through the forest and a tall rocky cliff blocked their way. Annette thumped down on the hard ground and leaned against the trunk of a lone spruce tree. Green-eyes turned and looked at her. He seemed worried she thought. Good, maybe Malloy and Henry would catch up to them. That would show him.

"We go."

"You go. I must rest." Annette closed her eyes. Though she was frightened, she was sure that the native wouldn't hurt her. He'd had plenty of chances to do that if he had wanted to. No, he was taking her somewhere, to the place where her father and brother were, of that she was sure. But Annette was exhausted. She couldn't have managed another step. It would just have to wait. She closed her eyes and fell instantly asleep.

Green-eyes listened carefully. He knew the white men were following. It would not be long. He couldn't risk getting caught. He'd been instructed to bring the foreign girl. The consequences of failure scared him. No one upset the Queen. Green-eyes scooped up Annette's slender form and draped her over his shoulder. Carrying her like a sack of potatoes, the native continued along the base of the cliff.

Annette dreamed. There were times she seemed to float. Her head whirled and she felt as if she were falling through clouds. When she landed it was dark. Annette felt cold and damp and saw herself going down a long, dark tunnel. There was light at the end of the tunnel, a blazing yellow light, and heat. Annette opened her eyes. She saw grass. It was dusk. She heard the heavy breathing of her captor.

He must've sensed she'd awaken. Green-eyes put her down. Annette looked around. They were in a boulder-pitted meadow. Tall, scantily treed granite cliffs with jagged snow-capped mountain peaks surrounded them. Below in the forested valley she saw the flickering lights of what she presumed were a village.

"Come. We not far. The Queen awaits," said Green-eyes.

"The Queen? The Queen of what..or where?" asked Annette. She walked slowly. "Where are we?"

"Home. This our village. Queen wants you. Let's go." Green-eyes started marching across the sloping meadow.

The village, scattered among a maze of dirt paths in a small clearing, was a conglomeration of rectangular and round log cabins with thatched roofs. It had a very distinct Scandinavian look. It reminded Annette of northern Viking villages that she had seen in picture books. It was not what she had expected. She had presumed that since her captors were natives, that the village or camp would be Indian. Fires were lit in many of the cabins and smoke poured out the chimneys. Through one cabin window, Annette caught a glimpse of some human figures sitting at a table eating.. Occasionally she heard a dog bark. There was no telling how large the village was, and Annette saw nothing that looked like any kind of commercial street. She wondered exactly where she was going. The village seemed to be thinning out and forest was beginning to close in.

Green-eyes took her left arm and guided her into a road to the right of the one they were travelling on. This one was paved with flat stones. It widened out into a courtyard. Annette gasped. A huge three-story stone and wood castle complete with turrets at either of the front corners blocked their path.

They went up the front steps, which were made of polished flat stone. The front double doors each had a huge golden doorknocker mounted midway on them. Green-eyes used one of them to knock on the door. Annette trembled. It was getting cold. They stood a minute or two in silence. The door opened. A tall, broad shouldered, dark-haired, bearded white man opened the door. Green-eyes thrust Annette towards the man, nodded, then turned and walked away.

The man who had answered the door smiled at Annette. He ushered her inside.

"This way m'lady. You're surely tired after your long and arduous journey. I will arrange for a bath and a meal to be brought to you."

"You speak English! Who are you?" Annette allowed herself to be led inside. An oil lamp dimly lit the entranceway. It was made of dark polished stone.

"I am a Caretaker. My name is Hubert. Come this way. After you finished your toilet, the Queen wishes to see you. Please follow me."

Annette followed Hubert down a long dimly torch lit hall. The polished stone of the entranceway gave way to polished hardwood. Closed doorways led off this main hall. The hallway opened into a large room. A woven tapestry hung along part of one wall and extended near its full length. Annette noticed that the tapestry seemed to be a map. She saw the European continent, the islands of Greenland and Iceland, and a crude, partial inaccurate map of North America. This main room had a high ceiling and lanterns dotted the walls at regular intervals. There were a few bearskin rugs on the floor and scattered arrangements of tables and chairs were clustered about. The furniture was made of carved wood. At one end of the room was a finely crafted decorated dark wood staircase that lead to the balcony surrounding the main hall. Doors dotted the balcony hall at intervals. Hubert led Annette up the stairway. They walked along the left side of the balcony. Hubert stopped at a door. From his pocket he withdrew a ring of iron keys, selected one and unlocked the door. He gestured for Annette to enter.

"I'll have hot water drawn for your bath Miss." The door closed, and Annette heard the lock click into place.

The walls were whitewashed and a painting of a French farm scene hung over the small fireplace. A fire was burning, and a lantern on a table next to the four-poster bed gave enough light for Annette to see her surroundings. A wooden closet sat across from the bed. Annette went to it and opened it. There were a few blouses, and some long black woollen skirts hanging in it. Against the wall opposite the bed was a window. A wooden rocking chair sat nearby. Annette went to the window. Annette noticed that an intricate iron lacework prevented the window from fully opening out. She looked out into the gloom. The moon was high overhead. The silhouetted mountains loomed around the castle.

Annette turned and walked to bed and lay down. She felt the tension ease and weariness overcame her. A knock on the door startled her.

"Who is it?"

"Mary. I have your bath water."

Annette heard the door unlock. It opened. A white girl in her late teens and dressed in a doeskin skirt and white cotton blouse entered. She carried two large wooden pails of steaming water on a wood brace balanced on her back. Hubert entered behind her carrying a large tin bath. He placed it near the fireplace, then stepped back, blocking the doorway. Mary poured the water into the tub. From her pocket she took a bar of soap and put it on the floor next to the tub. "I will bring towels for you in a moment." She curtsied, and then left. Hubert smiled at Annette. "I will bring Ma'amselle her dinner shortly. Enjoy."

Now left alone, Annette undressed and eased herself into the tub. She leaned back and let the water cover her. Annette felt the tension leave her. Tired, she closed her eyes and fell asleep.

***

Malloy and Colton dragged the canoe containing their silent captive ashore. Despite a variety of threats, Malloy still couldn't elicit any information from the prisoner. It was just chance that Colton had spotted a corner of the hidden canoe in some bush near the shore.

"Don't tell me. We have to take him with us. Right?" asked Colton, thumbing their prisoner.

"We don't have a choice. We can't afford to turn him loose. Besides, he may give something away yet," replied Malloy as he stooped down to study the tracks. He stretched and looked at the forest. "They went in there. There seems to be an animal path. They're probably following that."

"Where do you think he's taking Annette?"

"If I knew that, I'd be there ahead of him. There are no known Indian villages up this way. But that doesn't mean there isn't one. We'll just keep following as best we can. They have to stop soon."

Malloy turned and hauled the native out of the canoe. "Come on, you're gonna get some exercise." Malloy took some rope from his pack, cut off a six-foot length, and using a slipknot tied one end around the Indian's neck. He wrapped the other end around his hand. "Let's go."

The small party started off with Malloy leading the native. Colton walked in the rear. He carried Malloy's rifle, causally aimed at the Indian's back.

The trees were thick and the plant vegetation lush. The trail, if it could be called that, was invisible at times. Thistles and thorns scratched their arms. Little sunlight was able to pierce the dense foliage. It was cool and Colton noted with relief that the flies and mosquitoes seemed to be at a minimum. The only thing unnatural was the lack of wildlife. It was strangely silent in the woods. Their boots crunched over old sticks and brush, sounding unusually loud.

An uneasy feeling crept over Malloy. He glanced back at his captive. The Indian's face revealed neither emotion nor interest in his surroundings. Malloy kept his eyes moving.

Late in the afternoon they entered a clearing. A sheer jagged cliff wall blocked their passage. Malloy stopped. He examined the cliff face. "I doubt they went up there. There must be a break along the wall somewhere. I'll tie Chief No-Tongue here to a tree, then we'll scout around."

Malloy gestured for the native to sit at the base of a pine tree. He then securely bound the prisoner. He stepped back and inspected his work. "That should hold you." He turned to Colton. "Come on."

The two men followed the cliff face east. Looking up, Malloy could see its forested top. He noted that although the rock face was jagged, there were few handholds. They continued on for a while longer, but the cliff face showed no sign of descending.

"Let's try the other way," said Malloy. The men turned around and went back. Malloy stopped briefly checking on their captive. The Indian remained bound to the tree. He sat impassively. Malloy indicated through sign language that he would feed the man when they returned.

"Everything okay?" asked Colton.

"Yep, he's not going anywhere."

Going west, the cliff wall decayed. Forest and undergrowth made for easy handholds so that Malloy and Colton could ascend. They worked their way northwest, climbing higher. Colton looked out and saw nothing but dense forest descending over the land like green carpet.

"Henry, come here," called Malloy.

Colton broke from his reverie and saw Malloy standing about fifteen feet away. Colton scrambled over.

"What is it?"

"A trail. And I found this." He held up a piece of red and black-chequered cloth.

"It's from Annette's shirt."

"Yep. I found it sticking to a bush up there." Malloy pointed towards some dense brush." The Indian's carrying her."

"Let's go."

"Not so fast. It's getting dark. We can't follow the trail at night, and if we use torches, they'll see us coming. No, We'll make camp, and follow the trail in the morning."

"They could be miles away," countered Colton.

"I doubt it. I've a feeling it's not that far."

The two men returned to their camp. The Indian was gone. Malloy cursed. He ran over to the tree and examined the ropes. "They've been cut," he announced.

"His friends came."

Colton clutched the rifle and looked around. "What do we do?"

"Have dinner and take a few precautions. They'll be back."

Colton gathered wood for a fire. Malloy cooked a supper of tea, biscuits and beans. They ate in silence.

"Time to turn in."

"You're going to sleep?" asked Colton incredulously.

"One of us is, the other will take watch. Get your bedroll out."

They returned at night to the campsite. They watched silently from the forest at the dying embers of the fire and the two shadowed forms lying quietly. They had wanted to kill the white men in revenge for their fallen comrade, but the Queen wouldn't allow it. She told them she needed these men and to bring them to her. She promised that justice would be done.

Silently they crept into the camp, clubs and ropes ready. They had been warned that these men were fierce warriors, and that they carried white man's weapons. Two men stepped forward toward each of the sleeping victims. One man would pull the cover off, the other would render their prey unconscious. The two braves pulled the blankets back simultaneously and gasped!

"That's enough boys," drawled Malloy and he fired over their heads. The two men with clubs turned swiftly. "Drop' em."

The gunshot woke Colton, who'd fallen asleep while being on watch from the other side of the camp. He thrashed and stumbled into the camp, clumsily clutching the rifle. "What's going.."

Two of the Indians tackled him.

"Oh shit!" Malloy took aim and shot one of the Indians. The other two hurled their clubs at him. One of the clubs hit his arm. Malloy dropped his revolver. As he bent down to pick it up, the two men rushed him. They went down in a pile.

Colton lashed out against his attackers. He caught one man in the stomach. It was like hitting a brick wall. The other attacker launched a series of punches at Colton hitting him in the torso and face. The blows blinded Colton. He fought as best he could, but it wasn't enough. He stumbled and fell down. They were on him with ropes. In a matter of seconds Colton found himself trussed like a Thanksgiving turkey.

Meanwhile the other two natives were in trouble. Malloy knocked one of them unconscious with a well-aimed punch to the solar plexus. The other Indian was reeling under an onslaught of swift, pulverizing punches. Malloy heard a twig crack behind him. He ducked and whirled aside. A third Indian swooped down with a club, just missing his skull. Malloy hit the man on the back of his head with his fist. The Indian fell face first into the dirt. He shook himself off and pushed himself up. Just in time to catch a stunning left to his jaw. It propelled the man against a spruce tree, smacking his head. The second attacker, now recovered, moved in. He had picked up his fallen comrade's club. He swung at Malloy. Malloy sidestepped it and hit the man in the kidneys. The Indian grunted. Suddenly the last Native flung himself on Malloy's back. Malloy flipped him off; but in doing so, left himself open. The second Native hammer punched Malloy in the back of the head. Malloy, dazed, fell to his knees. And then they had him. Two men grabbed each arm, as the third swung the club. Sharp pain exploded in Malloy's head then faded into oblivion.

CHAPTER TWELVE: AUDIENCE WITH A QUEEN

"Miss?" whispered Mary.

Annette awoke with a start. The cool water of the bath sent a chill over her. She looked up to see the young servant holding two folded towels. Annette smiled. "I guess I fell asleep." She reached and took a towel. "Put the other over the chair."

"Yes Ma'amselle.' nodded Mary. "I brought some clothes for you. I am having your clothes laundered. Yours were very dirty and not suitable for an audience with our Queen."

"Thanks," replied Annette as she rose wrapping the towel around her. She stepped out of the tub and reached for the other towel. Annette noticed that clean undergarments, a long black skirt, white blouse and short black leather boots lay on the bed. She dressed, then sat and combed her hair. It felt good to be clean again. Her stomach growled. It had been sometime since she had eaten. Annette hoped that the Queen was planning to serve dinner.

Minutes passed. Finally Annette heard the lock on the door being turned. The door opened and Hubert poked his head in. He smiled. "The Queen is ready to see you. Please follow me."

They went downstairs and through one of the doors leading off from the main hall. This led to a short hallway. At the end of the hall was a set of double doors. Hubert opened them and they entered the throne room.

I've stepped back in time thought Annette. Wooden beams supported the high ceiling. Light came from candelabra above and lit torches posted on wooden pillars at regular intervals. Viking shields and spears lined the walls. There was one window at the end of the room above a fur-lined throne. On either side of the throne, dressed in traditional Viking garb stood two guards. As Annette walked closer, she saw that the muscular men were natives.

The Queen sat upon the throne. She wore a long woven white dress with gold and silver threads. Wrapped around her slender waist was a leather belt with a scabbard holding a short sword. A Viking helmet sat upon her head. Her long silver white hair framed her face. She had strong clean-cut features and the lightest blue eyes Annette had ever seen. Hubert stepped aside. Annette curtsied, then stood while the Queen examined her. There was no expression upon the monarch's face. Her icy eyes studied Annette. There was no sound. The silence made Annette afraid, but she dared not to speak.

"You have made a long journey," stated the Queen in French.

"You are the daughter of George Bouchard, the sister of Andre Bouchard?"

"Why yes, do you know where they are?" asked Annette. She felt her heart pound with excitement.

"Silence," ordered the Queen. "They are here. Why have you come?"

"To find them. To convince them to come home."

"That will not be possible, but you may see them-later. But first you and I will talk. I have many questions. Have you eaten?"

"No Your Highness."

The Queen turned to Hubert. "Inform the kitchen to prepare a meal for Miss Bouchard."

"Yes your Worship." The Queen turned back to Annette. "I speak several tongues. Do you prefer to converse in English or French?"

"Either."

"Then we shall continue in French. It is easier for me to express myself and for you to understand." The Queen stood up and gestured for Annette to follow her. She led Annette to a small sitting room off the throne room. A thick bearskin rug covered most of the floor. In the center were table and chairs. "Sit down."

Annette obeyed. The Queen sat down opposite her. There was a knock on the door and Hubert entered with a tray laden with cheeses, bread, fruit, two gold cups and a decanter of dark wine. He set the tray down and went silently out.

"Do you know why your father and brother came here?" asked the Queen.

"They were prospecting for gold. Father had lost our--fortune and was trying to regain it."

The Queen gestured for Annette to eat. "Men are always searching for fortunes. Few find what they seek. Some realize not what they have. On occasion, men have wandered into my realm. Most decided to stay. They realized that what we offered was more than what they had. Some caused problems. Those that break our rules are punished accordingly."

Annette spread some cheese on a chunk of bread and ate hungrily.

"Try some wine." The Queen poured her a cup.

"Thank you. Can you tell me, how are my father and brother?" Annette lifted the cup with a trembling hand and took a sip. The wine was sweet. Berry wine Annette decided.

"You will be allowed to see your father shortly. They wandered into our realm searching for gold. We fed them. Gave them shelter. Your father had hurt his ankle." The Queen sat back and watched Annette eat.

Annette nodded. "Thank you your Highness. I do not wish to be rude, but I am curious. How did you come here? The Viking shields, dress. Just where am I?"

For the first time, a smile crept upon the Queen's face. She removed her helmet and sat back in her chair. Annette noticed that she was younger then originally she had thought, though the character lines around her eyes and mouth indicated that she was probably in her forties.

"I am Freydis, Queen of Vinland. This place we call Asgard, because it's beauty is fit for the Gods. My people came here centuries ago. It was in the year 1342 of our Lord. My ancestors were from the new land we called Greenland. But the Church turned evil against us. We left there, seeking freedom from the tyranny. There was a storm. Several of the ships were blown off course. They built shelters and established a colony. The land was good. It is rich in game, fish and wild grains. The Beotuk and Algonquin Skraelings were friendly at first. They loved milk. We traded; but our men would not trade their women, and the skraelings valued those of us with yellow hair. War broke out. My people were no match for the skraelings, for they were many. Winter was coming. The seas were too stormy to traverse, so we moved inland. We travelled far and wide until coming here. The Nah'aa skraelings were friendly. Later, we made bonds with the mountain giants. And so we have remained. Others came later, French traders and priests. That is how we learned their tongue. One holy man stayed with us for a long time. He taught us many things. And then the English came. There was a man named McLeod whom my ancestor met oh- a hundred years or so ago. This man McLeod was a trader. He wanted furs. He did not know about our gold. And there was another Englishman named Campbell. It was through people like them and others that came that my few skraeling subjects, as well as some of my people, learned English. This too has been handed down. But others have also come. Not long ago, greedy, violent men came searching for gold. Some brought disease. There were many deaths, but we survived. We rarely bother with the outside world. There are Dene skraelings who trade with us. Through them we acquired new metals and tools. They bring us news of the outside world. And from what I have heard, it is better here, though of late I have seen strange flying machines in the skies. Do you know of this?"

"Those are aeroplanes. They carry mail and supplies to towns," said Annette.

"These devices are man-made? How do they work?"

"Mechanical motors give the aeroplanes power."

The Queen shook her head. "The world is indeed becoming a strange place with all these machines."

"When can I see my father and brother?" asked Annette.

"After you have eaten. Once you have seen them, we will talk more. You are an intelligent woman. I think there is much I can learn from you."

The Queen rose. "Finish your meal. Hubert will take you to see your father."

CHAPTER THIRTEEN: GEORGE BOUCHARD

After Freydis had left, Annette finished eating. She was ravenous. The cheese, bread and fruit tasted good. Her energy returned. There was a tap at the door and Hubert entered. Annette stood up.

"Come with me Miss."

Hubert led Annette back through the throne room, now empty, and down the hallway into the main room. They crossed the room and paused at a heavy wood door. Hubert removed an iron key ring from a pocket on his tunic, and unlocked the door. He lit the torch that was in a holder just inside the doorway. Their footsteps echoed as they descended a series of stone steps. The dungeon thought Annette.

Her deduction proved correct. Below them was a huge torchlit chamber filled with medieval torture devices. Several pokers lay resting in the burning embers of a stone fireplace. Against the far wall were a wooden rack, and several small iron cages. A guard sat at a table. He was a big brawny young man with dark skin, native facial features, light brown hair and green eyes. As the guards upstairs, he was dressed in a blue tunic, fur vest, leggings and fur boots. He looked up briefly. His eyes drank in Annette. He smiled. Getting no response, he turned sullenly away. They crossed the room. A hallway leading from the opposite wall led to the cells. In a cell on the right side of the corridor, there was a shuffling sound. Annette peered through the iron bars. Sitting on a bed of straw was a shadowed figure.

"Father!" cried Annette.

Dim light revealed a gaunt figure garbed in buckskin pants and a dirty white shirt struggling to stand. "Annette? Annette! How can this be? What are you doing here?"

Off the floor he picked up a stout wooden crutch. Annette gasped. Her father was missing his right foot. He looked down at his leg, then at his daughter. He hobbled across to the cell door. "They did what they could."

Tears crept into her eyes as Annette studied her father's face. She saw the deep haunted look in his eyes, protruding cheekbones of a once rounded face. A thick scraggly beard and shoulder length matted hair gave him a beast-like appearance. The hands that grasped the bars were dirty and calloused.

Annette turned to Hubert. "Why is my father here?" demanded Annette. She looked around. "Where is my brother?"

Hubert said nothing. He turned and walked away.

"Why are you imprisoned? Where is Andre?" demanded Annette.

"Dead," sobbed George Bouchard.   He stared into his daughter's violet eyes, took a deep breath and shook his head. "It's a long story."

Annette searched her father's face. "Tell me."

"What are you doing here Annette?"

"Searching for you. Mother died. I have no one else. Why did you leave us for so long? What happened to Andre?"

Annette turned to Hubert. "I wish to spend some time with my father. Is that allowed?"

"Yes, if you wish." Hubert unlocked the cell door. "Back." He ordered George Bouchard." He gestured for Annette to enter. "Yell when you're done and we'll take you back."

Annette entered and the door clanged shut behind her.

"Sit down. I'll explain." George Bouchard slumped to floor and leaned against the dank cell wall. "It is difficult to stand for any length of time these days."

Annette sat down cross-legged by the barred door. She patted her father's knee. Her father took her hand and squeezed it.

"Annette. Where do I begin? How do I apologize for what I put your mother and you through? How can I explain what I had hoped for? But you know I did it for us. I wanted us to have all the things we had when you were young. I was ashamed for you to grow up in poverty. Andre needed an education. I was too old to start a career again. The bank job gave us food, paid our rent, but there was nothing else. I always wanted the best for you and Andre." George Bouchard's eyes teared.

"It's okay father. I understand."

George Bouchard took a deep breath. "It began when I met Mr. Wilkinson at the club bar. We drank and talked. He told me that he was planning an expedition to the Northwest Territories. Gold had been discovered. He had been out west before. He told me that on an earlier visit he learned of a valley of gold. But it took hard work to prospect. He needed help mining it. We could be rich men he said. I was interested naturally, but I told him I didn't have the type of money he required, just a little bit I'd manage to tuck away. We talked some more. To make matters short, we worked out a deal and became partners."

"And you left."

George Bouchard met his daughter's gaze. "Yes, I left, with your brother. We travelled by train and then took a steamboat up the rivers to Fort Simpson. There we outfitted ourselves and travelled the Laird and the Nahanni rivers. It was a gruelling journey, one of the boats upset and we lost some of our supplies. It took us longer than we expected."

"But you did arrive," said Annette. She smiled at her father.

"Yes, we arrived. We found an abandoned cabin near the Flat River and set up camp. It was early fall. We also discovered that Wilkinson's funds were depleted. He had lied to us. He was as desperate as we were. So, we did some trapping. None of us were too good at it. We barely made enough to keep the supplies stocked. We kept to ourselves; other than a few trappers or the odd prospector we had little contact with anyone. Finally, I asked Wilkinson about this valley of gold. He hesitated a bit at first. I think he was not quite trustful of us, and too, he was a bit scared. After all, he knew about these Vikings," gestured George Bouchard. "We did not." Annette's father stopped and took a deep breath.

"Are you all right?"

George patted his daughter's hand. "It is nothing. I'm fine. Now where was I?"

"The Vikings?"

"Yes, as I said, we knew nothing of them. Anyway we survived until spring. Then we set out again. We travelled to the end of Irvine Creek, and hiked inland until we came to the mountain. We had approached it from the north side, so of course this place was hidden from us. Wilkinson showed us the hidden mine entrance. We began prospecting. And we found gold!" George Bouchard's eyes glittered. "He hadn't lied. Nuggets as big as a man's fist!

Late one afternoon Wilkinson and your brother Andre went hunting. I was back at camp, starting to prepare supper. Suddenly they came running into camp. Your brother had been wounded in his arm. His clothes were torn and bloody. Wilkinson screamed, ' They're after us. We must leave.' And then they were upon us. I had never seen such barbarians. We barely escaped. We ran to the cave. From there our position was good. We had rifles. They didn't. We killed several of them. But what we didn't know was that there was a tunnel connecting our mine with theirs. I have since discovered that the mountain is maze of tunnels. That night they launched a surprise attack. We fought, but these men were too powerful for us. I was wounded by a battleaxe and knocked unconscious. When I woke up, I was here, imprisoned. Their doctor or shaman attended to us. The cut from the axe was too deep. There was nothing he could do. My foot was amputated."

"Then what happened?" prodded Annette.

"We were brought before the Queen Freydis. It turns out that Wilkinson and Andre had come upon their hunting party. Andre, in fear, accidentally shot Dansa's son."

"They killed Andre," said Annette. Tears welled in her eyes as she stared at the cold damp floor.

"Yes, they killed him. Poor Andre! He paid dearly for his mistake. They tortured him. His screams haunted my days and nights, and still do," whispered George Bouchard.

"Oh father! How horrible!" Annette wept. Tears streaked her face She and Andre had been close. The thought of her brother being tortured was beyond her. She couldn't fathom the logic in it. Annette shivered. She was scared. Her thoughts turned to Malloy and Colton. They were their only hope. She told her father about them.

"I wish them luck, though I doubt there's much even they can do," said George Bouchard.

Father and daughter sat in silence. Time passed by. Footsteps crunched on the stone. The door lock clanked. Annette looked up. The guard stood over her. He smiled at her.

"You bastard! Let my father go!" hissed Annette. She stood up.

"He is an old man. Why are you doing this? Take me to Queen Freydis."

The guard cocked his head and smiled at her. He moved closer to her. "You have spirit I like that in a woman."

"Don't you lay a hand on me. I'll tell the Queen."

The guard laughed. "The Queen is my mother."

Annette's jaw dropped. This was a prince? A prison guard? Annette couldn't understand it. She took another step back. She was against the stone wall. A torch flickered in a holder above her. She reached up and snatched the torch down. She brandished it in front of her.

The guard stepped back and drew his broadsword. "Put it back. I would hate to kill you."

"You wouldn't dare."

He glanced at George Bouchard. "Perhaps. Then perhaps you would like to see your father tortured and killed. Just like I did your brother."

"You bastard!" cried George Bouchard. He swung at the guard. The door slammed in his face. His hands snaked out to grip the bars and keep himself from falling. His face pressed against the bars.
Annette flung the torch at the guard. He sidestepped swiftly and grabbed Annette's arm. It was like being caught in an iron vice.

Annette struggled. She slapped his face. He caught her hand as she tried to hit him again.

The guard tossed his head back and laughed louder "Let her go!" bellowed George Bouchard. His fist slammed against the door in frustration.

CHAPTER FOURTEEN: IMPRISONED

Pain brought Malloy back to consciousness. His head ached and his arms were numb. He felt soft grass beneath him. Malloy opened his eyes and discovered that he was tied with thick ropes. The sun was setting. He'd been out for some time. Colton lay about six feet away bound hand and foot. Malloy noticed that Colton was sporting a nasty bruise on the right side of his face, and that his lower lip was cut. A shadow crossed over Malloy. He looked up and to his right. The Indian he had nicknamed Green-eyes stood over him. But behind Green-eyes were--Vikings? Malloy shook his head in disbelief. There were four of them, dressed in what Malloy assumed as fairly typical garb or at least what Malloy recognized from reading Prince Valliant in the funnies. They were big, muscular men of average height, with the exception of Green-eyes who Malloy assumed was their leader. If Malloy wasn't really awake, then he was hallucinating. It was like stepping back into the past.

"You are a brave warrior," said Green-eyes.

"So, you do speak English," said Malloy. "Who are your friends?"

He nodded at the Vikings.

"You'll find out." Green-eyes turned to the Vikings. One of them came forward. He was a tall strapping young man with broad shoulders. His face was long with high cheekbones and a broken nose. His eyes were icy blue, and his lank hair blond. It cascaded to his shoulders. A headband kept the hair away from his face. He wore a leather vest and deerskin trousers tucked into knee leggings with moccasins. A thick leather belt with a scabbard for a short broad sword was around his waist. He bent over and cut the bonds around Malloy's ankles. "Stand up."

Malloy struggled to his feet. Two of the blond Viking's friends hauled Colton to his feet. Like Malloy, his bonds were cut so he could walk.

"I take it, we're going with you," said Malloy.

"Yes. Do not try to escape. You will be killed," replied the blond Viking.

Malloy noted that one of the Vikings, a husky brown-haired lad of maybe twenty-carried Malloy's rifle and pistol. Malloy wondered if the fellow knew how to use them.

They started walking in single file along the cliff wall. Green-eyes and the blond Viking were leading. Then came Malloy, another Viking, Colton, and the last two northern barbarians. A narrow deer trail started up the cliff. They followed this. At times strong hands gripped Malloy to keep him from slipping. They rounded a bend and stopped at a narrow cave entrance. Green-eyes and the Viking went in. It was a tight fit for the blond Viking, and an even tighter fit for Malloy. Green-eyes stood with a lit torch. Malloy noticed an iron torch holder on the wall. The passage widened out and they walked slowly. Malloy noticed that parts of the tunnel had been dug out and stout beams braced parts of the wall and roof. Their footsteps echoed softly. They stopped once to rest. Malloy and Colton were given water from a bag made from a goat's stomach.

"Who are these guys?" whispered Colton. They were sitting on the cold stone floor.

"I assume we'll find out. They're not too talkative right now. But I don't think we're daydreaming. This is for real," said Malloy. "But I'll make you a bet that we'll find Annette and what happened to her father's expedition. I think they're the key to the mystery of this region."

Green-eyes came over and offered them some beef jerky. Malloy thanked him and took a bite from the piece that had been offered. Colton declined.

"You should've taken the food," said Malloy.

"The stuff's too tough to chew," said Colton.

"It'll give you energy. You'll need it," Malloy's eyes followed Green-eyes. He had walked over to the blond Viking and the two men were talking. Malloy strained his ears, but he couldn't hear what was said.

A few minutes later both he and Colton were hauled to their feet, and the party took off again into the stygian darkness. Finally, Malloy noticed another light ahead, but this light was steady. Soon they were through the tunnel and outside. It was dark now, but silhouetted in the moonlight he could see mountainous ridges and forest. Down below was a clearing. The lights of a village glimmered. Malloy guess that that was their destination. He wondered where they were. He hadn't known that any town or village existed in this region.

****

"Let her go!" bellowed George Bouchard.

The Viking prince threw his head back and laughed.

"THAT'S QUITE ENOUGH ERIC," boomed a female voice.

The Viking turned and saw his Queen mother and two guards. He turned his head again and looked at Annette. "Later," he hissed as he let go of her arms.

Annette ran to the Queen. "Thank you."

"I'm afraid my son can't control his amorous impulses. However he does need a wife. You might be able to civilize him. But we will talk of that later," said Freydis. She smiled coldly at Annette.

"My father!" Annette turned and looked at her father who stood clutching the iron bars of the cell door.

"Yes, we must speak of him and Mr. Wilkinson." Freydis glanced at the prisoners' cells, and then turned back to Annette. " It is not so simple. They violated our laws."

"You killed my brother," stated Annette.

"Your brother killed my youngest son" spat Queen Freydis.

"But it was an accident."

"So that is what your father told you?" Freydis cast her gaze towards George Bouchard's cell. "Well, that may be what he believes. Come."

Two guards stepped on either side of Annette or the entourage left the dungeon. As they walked through the doorway, Annette glanced back. Eric was watching her. He smiled at her.

Once in the throne room, Freydis returned to her chair. A messenger waited for her. He was a short, husky bearded man. He bowed. Fredyis gestured for the man to come forward.

"What is it Thorfinn?" asked the Queen in a language Annette didn't recognize.

"Bjarni's party returns with two prisoners. Strangers from the outside."

"Put them in the dungeon. I will see them tomorrow." She turned to Annette. "You travelled with two men companions?"
Annette nodded affirmatively.

"They are being brought here. You will see them tomorrow. I think it best you rest for now." Freydis looked at one of the guards. He came forward.

"Escort our guest to her room."

The Guard bowed. "Yes, your highness."

Annette stared at the Queen for a moment; they reluctantly went with the guard.

Back in her room, Annette paced across the floor. She had to see Malloy and Henry. But how? Her door was locked. She was as much a prisoner as they. There seemed little she could do at the moment.

When she thought about her father, crippled and lying in the filthy dungeon, tears poured out her eyes and streamed her cheeks. Her brother Andre was dead. What kind of justice was this? The thought of Andre killing anyone escaped her. Andre had been a sensitive young man, full of life and humor. If he had killed, it must have been in self-defense. Of this she was certain.

She had seen Wilkinson too, across from her father's cell, staring out at her. A tall, gaunt skeleton of a man with large crazy dark eyes, he frightened her. And yet, there had been something familiar about him. Annette shook her head. Now that was crazy. She'd never met the man. She'd never laid eyes on him until this moment. Of course with all the filth and the beard and the long hair, it was hard to even recognize him as a human being.

A knock at the door brought her out of her revelry. "Yes?"

"It is Mary," said a muffled voice. "I have some tea. Queen Freydis said you might like some."

"Thank you."

Annette heard the door unlock. Hubert stood outside. Mary entered. On a wooden tray was an empty cup and pot of tea. She set this down on the small table by the bed. "Good night." She curtsied.

"Good night," replied Annette.

Mary left the room and Annette heard Hubert lock the door. She sat on the bed and poured herself a cup of tea. It tasted of mint. Annette relaxed and leaned against a pillow. There had to be a way out.

***

As they came closer to town, Malloy heard dogs barking. The village had a distinct old European look. He wondered how Vikings got here. They were herded through town and towards a large stone and wood building with two turrets.

"The palace," said the blond Viking, who now walked next to Malloy.

"Very impressive."

"Take a good look. It will be the last time you see its outside," said their blond captor.

They entered the building by a side entrance and were escorted downstairs. A short passage led to a larger room. It was filled with medieval torture devices. They walked through this and down another corridors where iron barred cells lined the walls. Colton and Malloy's bonds were cut as they were thrown into one of the cells.

"Company Wilky," said a voice.

Colton picked himself up off the floor. He rushed towards the cell door, but it closed with a loud clang. "Bastards!" He cursed.

"They are that and more," said the voice.

Colton pushed himself against the bars. "Who is this?"

"A fellow prisoner like yourself. My name is George."

"Annette's father?" he asked.

"The same unfortunate man. You must be Henry. Annette told me about you."

"You've seen her?"

"Yes. She's a prisoner here too. But with better quarters."

"Where are we?" asked Colton.

"You're in hell," he cackled.

Malloy picked himself up off the cold stone floor. He rubbed his arms. The circulation was just returning. He swung them around and practiced bending them. Within a few minutes he felt better. He leaned against the black iron bars.

"Mr. Bouchard? My name's Duke Malloy. You're daughter hired me to find you. Are you all right?"

"As well as can be expected. I talked to my daughter just moments ago."

"Annette's here!" cried Colton. He stopped pacing and ran to the cell bars.

"Yes. Luckily the Queen has taken a fancy to her."

"What do you mean?" asked Malloy. But the only reply he got was silence.

Another voice from across the hall replied, "I wouldn't" worry about her my old chappie. It's yerself you need be concerned with."

"The elusive Mr. Wilkinson I presume," said Malloy.

"Correct."

"There's some Mounties that'd like a word with you," said Malloy.

"I don't doubt it. The truth is these barbarians are responsible for my former companions' doom. I escaped, but was later taken captive."

"My son Andre," said Bouchard. "They tortured and killed him." He sobbed.

I'm sorry to hear that," said Malloy.

"Who are these people?" asked Colton.

"Descendents of Viking explorers. They've carved themselves a nice little kingdom in this godforsaken territory. And they're filthy rich, but seem not to care," said Wilkinson.

"You're referring to the tales about the valley of gold, or lost gold mine," said Malloy.

"Indeed I am. It exists. I've seen it with my own eyes. The problem is that it's already claimed," said Wilkinson.

"But knowing that, you came back," said Malloy.

"Yes. Greed. Sheer greed. Man's greatest folly, sir. And for that I'm paying dearly. You see I barely escaped last time. And now, well, I suspect my days are numbered."

"We've got to get out of here!" cried Colton. He and grasped the bars, and shook them. They didn't budge.

"There is no escape," whispered Bouchard. "Only death."

His remark put a somber mood over all. Malloy sat down in a pile of straw that lay in the corner. He closed his eyes and rested. There was nothing to do now. He'd have to find out more first, and then wait for a chance. He thought of Annette. At least she was safe.

CHAPTER FIFTEEN: CRIME AND PUNISHMENT

Footsteps crunched on the stone floor. Malloy opened his eyes. There was a jingling of keys. The door creaked open. A dim flickering stream of light illuminated the cell. He looked up. Two guards stood in the doorway. One of them held two bowls of steaming food. The one holding the bowls took two paces inside and put the bowls down on the floor. He withdrew and cell was locked again.

"Hey Colton, wake up. Room service has brought our breakfast," said Malloy, as he gave Colton a gentle push with his foot.

"Huh?" groaned Colton. He rolled over. His eyes peered out. "Uh- I'm not dreaming am I?"

A face appeared at the cell door. "Eat. Queen Freydis wishes to see you."

"You speak English too, do you?" commented Malloy. He crawled over and looked at the bowls. Porridge. "No spoons?"

The face disappeared and he heard the guards walked away.

Malloy passed a bowl to Colton.

"What is this stuff?" he asked.

"Breakfast. Shut up and eat. We've an audience with the Queen."

"So I hear."

Malloy tipped the bowl and poured a bit of porridge into his mouth. It was lukewarm. He tasted several different grains, and while it might not suit his preference, at least it was nourishing.

***

Annette woke up with sunlight streaming through her window. Despite the thoughts of her brother's death and her father in a dungeon, the knowledge that at least he was alive comforted her. Her stress had given way to fatigue and Annette had simply passed out on the bed.
She flung off her covers and stretched. Using the pitcher and basin on the table next to the bed, Annette washed and changed her clothes. Then she sat and waited for someone to come and bring her breakfast.

***

The guards returned to escort Malloy and Colton to Queen Freydis. As they strode down the prison hall, Wilkinson called out to them, "Good luck chaps. Hope to see you again."

"That doesn't sound very promising," muttered Colton, who eyed Wilkinson as they passed his cell.

"Silence," ordered one of the guards, and gave Colton a poke in the back with his lance.

"Ow." Colton gave the guard a dirty look. That was another score to settle.

They entered the Throne Room. Malloy noted with interest the shields and lances that decorated the room. They were authentic. Both men were ordered to kneel on the floor in front of the throne.

"When our Queen Freydis enters, bow," said one guard.

Minutes passed by. Malloy knew that this was a psychological ploy to let them sweat it out. He sat calmly on his knees, studying the room. He knew that all the information he discovered would aid in their escape.

A door opened to the chamber and Malloy watched as Queen Freydis entered. She was a statuesque mature blonde haired woman. The Queen wore a long white dress, purple cape and a helmet with Rams' horns protruding from the front. Soft brown leather boots encased her feet. Malloy glanced at Colton and the men bowed. This seemed to please the Queen. She smiled. Her eyes paused on Malloy.

"You may rise."

Malloy lifted his head and stood up. One of the guards came forward, but Queen Freydis gestured and he backed away. Freydis leaned forward. Her eyes seemed to burn right through Malloy.

"What are you called?" asked Freydis.

"Duke Malloy. This is Henry David Colton. We're friends of Annette Bouchard," said Malloy.

"I know. We've been expecting you. I've been told you are a fierce warrior." The Queen sat back in her throne.

"A man is always fierce when defending his life and those of others," replied Malloy.

"Well put." Freydis nodded perceptibly. "You are looking for George Bouchard and James Wilkinson, yes?"

"That's what I was hired to do."

"Ah, a mercenary. Good." Queen Freydis allowed a smile to pass her lips.

"And now that you have found them?"

"First I'd like to know why they are imprisoned, said Malloy, "If it's not serious I ask that we be allowed to leave peacefully your Highness."

Queen Freydis' expression grew grim. "You are bold. However, I shall answer your question. They are responsible for killing my son. They stole gold from my treasury. Would you admit that both are serious crimes?"

"Yes. I'm sorry. I wasn't aware of the circumstances. What is there punishment?"

"One was executed. At the moment Bouchard and Wilkinson work the mine. They were so anxious to get my gold, I let them mine it --for me."

"How long is their sentence? I will not argue on Wilkinson's behalf. From what I learned, he was warned the last time. But surely George Bouchard has suffered enough. His son forfeited his life for your son's," said Malloy.

"Silence," ordered Freydis. "Even bold men must learn when to curb their tongues." The Queen raised her eyebrows and a cold smile swept across her face. "And now, I must decide what to do with you."

"What crimes have we committed?" demanded Colton. He was getting impatient. Malloy was doing nothing but sucking up to this female barbarian. The woman had the same tone and standing as his mother. Colton knew that a firm stand would do more. Someone needed to put her in her place.

"Colton, shut up!" muttered Malloy.

Colton turned angrily to Malloy. "I will not. This woman needs to be put in her place." He turned to the Queen. "Now you release my fiancée and her father immediately, or you'll find out just what twentieth century technology can do. You and your backwards kingdom will be wiped out!"

Two guards grabbed Colton's arms. He struggled an arm loose and punched one guard in the nose. The other guard hit Henry behind his knees with the staff of his lance. Colton legs gave out and he fell.

"Enough!" thundered Queen Freydis. "Take him back to the dungeon and teach him some manners."

The guards dragged Colton from the room.

"You refuse to aid your friend," said Queen Freydis.

"He could use a few manners," smiled Malloy.

The Queen rose. "Come with me Duke Malloy." She stepped down off the dais and walked over to him. She took his arm and led him out of the room. A guard followed discreetly behind. They walked down a hall and the Queen stopped at a door. The guard opened it.

"See we are not disturbed," she said to the guard.

Malloy found himself inside the Queen's private room. It was long, with beamed ceilings and windows along one side that looked out at the mountain. A wooden table with four chairs were placed near a stone fireplace at one end of the room. Next to the fireplace was a huge tin bathtub. It was filled with steaming water. At the other end of the room were a huge four-poster bed, a clothes closet, writing desk and chair. Woven tapestry's depicting Viking raids and battles hung along one wall. Bearskin rugs covered the floor.

Queen Freydis removed her helmet and placed it on the table. She untied her cape and laid it over the chair. She turned and faced Malloy.

She was an attractive woman with full, firm breasts and a just a hint of stomach. Her blond-white hair had a bit of a natural curl and framed her oval shaped face. The pale blue eyes were alive with passion. A wicked grin crept across her thin lips.

"Don't worry. I will not bite you," she whispered.

Malloy grinned. He knew what she wanted. And he knew what would happen if she didn't get it or was disappointed. The risk was too great. Virtue was not a problem, but he didn't like using people. However, in this instance it might prove to be a way to gain freedom for the others.

"Come here," whispered Freydis.

Malloy walked over to her. Her arms wrapped around his neck. She pulled his head down. Their lips crushed together. She kissed him fiercely, with urgency, snaking her tongue into his mouth. Quick hard kisses pelted his face. He responded in kind. Malloy's hands massaged Freydis' sides and back. He squeezed her buttocks. She pressed herself into him. He felt her breasts against his chest. He pulled her dress up over her head, took a step back and flung it on the floor. She stood naked before him. Her breasts were rounded with large erect nipples. Her stomach was still taunt, the hair between her thighs slightly darker than on her head. She moved closer to him and slowly undid the buttons on his shirt. Her slender strong hands caressed his hairy chest then slipped down and undid his belt and unbuttoned his trousers.

***

Henry David Colton, naked, huddled in a ball in a corner of his cell. He fought back the tears from the pain. His back and buttocks were torn with gashes from the lashing. Blood seeped from the wounds and stained the floor. His wrists were chaffed, and arms ached from being suspended in chains. He heard the cell door open. He opened his eyes. A guard threw his clothes in. He crawled over to them. Slowly he dressed himself. They will pay for this vowed Colton. They will pay for the indignity and pain they inflicted. His eyes burned with anger.

"You okay Mr. Colton?" asked Bouchard from his cell.

"I'm alive," croaked Colton. His throat was dry.

"It don't do to get them riled," said Wilkinson.

"Thanks for the advice," cracked Henry. He tried standing. His legs wobbled and he leaned against the cold stone wall for support. The cool dampness of the stones numbed the back pain. He sidestepped over to the cell door and peered out. Wilkinson stood in the cell across from him. Henry David Colton smiled at his fellow inmate, as he plotted Wilkinson's murder.

***

The door opened. Hubert entered with a tray of bread, cheese and fruit. He placed the tray on the table.

"Thank you," said Annette.

"You're welcome Miss," replied the servant.

"Am I to be kept in here all day? I would like some fresh air."

"I'll see what can be done," said Hubert as he left.

Annette ate hungrily. The rest and food revived her spirits. She thought about Malloy and Henry. She longed to see them. Maybe the Queen would allow her to visit them.

A key turned in the lock. Annette looked up as the door opened. She gasped. Eric stood in the doorway. He smiled at her. "I have come to take you outside," he said.

***

"You are a good lover Duke Malloy," said Freydis. She lay back against a pillow in the feather mattress bed. A look of relaxed contentment eased the years from her face.

"Glad you enjoyed it," said Malloy. The bath had felt good, but the lovemaking that followed was a bit too wild for his tastes. His back was sore from the deep furrows her nails made, and there were tiny bite marks on his shoulders. His head rested on a second pillow. He glanced over at Freydis, his eyes roving up from her naked breasts.

"So, what are your plans for us?" he asked casually.

The Queen smiled. "Perhaps I shall keep you for my consort. The others can work in the mine."

"And the woman, Annette Bouchard?" Malloy turned and looked up at the canopy.

"It is time my son marry. He needs a wife to calm him. She is educated. There is much she can teach us. Do you care for her?"

"No." Freydis studied Malloy's profile. The man masks his emotions well she thought, but it didn't matter. She was Queen. And she presumed that he valued his life and his manhood.

CHAPTER SIXTEEN: CAVERN OF GOLD

Annette was nervous. So far, Eric had been very polite but she didn't trust him. They had toured the village. From what Annette gathered, there was some communal farming and fishing done among the people of Asgard and the natives. Annette guessed that the population was somewhere around one hundred. There were few white women; most were mixed race, and even fewer children. The men she was told hunted and fished, while the women farmed in a nearby valley. The natives lived in their own community nearby. Many of the children had distinct native features. She and Eric were walking in a small garden area behind the palace. Birds were chirping in the trees and a gentle breeze rustled the leaves and flowers. Annette thought about Malloy and Henry.

Eric grabbed her wrist. He led her to some purple flowers. He bent over and picked one and gave it to her. Annette took it.

"Thank you."

Eric blushed. This behaviour was foreign to him. Women were always there for him. The girl at the pub gave herself freely, as did a few others he knew; but his mother had lectured him that night about how to court a woman. He found the woman called Annette attractive, though she wasn't quite as buxom as he would have preferred. She did have a certain grace about her movements, and she was intelligent. Not that it mattered to him. One didn't need to be smart to keep a house and have children. She had spirit though, and Eric intended to conquer it. And that thought brought a smile to his face. Now all he wanted was to plunge his manhood into her.

"Shall we walk Moreno?" he asked her in halting English. "I would show you our gold mine."

Annette had a no on her lips; she then stopped. Her curiosity gave in. She suddenly wanted to see what everyone was willing to die for. "Okay," she said, "Let's go see the mine."

Eric nodded and led her down a path that joined the main road leading out of the village. They continued to follow the narrowing path. It was pleasant walking through the forest of willow, aspen and spruce trees. The forest thinned out and gave way to a wide green meadow. As they ascended the mountains, dwarf birch replaced the grass. The hiking was harder. The trail soon narrowed. It led up and around the rugged mountains. There was still snow on some of the peaks. Far off she saw something glistening in the sunlight. She pointed to it and asked Eric, "What is that?"

"The ice mountain." replied Eric, "Don't worry about it. Watch your step."

They climbed higher. Looking up she could see a small crevice in the side of the mountain.

"That's the entrance," said Eric.

They stopped. Her brow was beaded with sweat. Her heartbeat was faster. Eric took a deep breath. The brief climb hadn't affected him at all. He stepped around her and entered the crevice. Annette followed.

Eric took a torch that was burning in a holder just inside the short, narrow passageway. Annette's hiking boots crunched the small pebbles and grit underneath. A cool dampness surrounded them. They walked for a minute or two and then the torch's light was lost in a huge cavern. Stalactites hung down like vampire teeth.

"Watch your step. Stay close behind," said Eric.

They walked along a well-worn path. The flickering torch made inhuman monsters of their shadows along the cavern wall. Annette shivered. The rocky walls fell away as the path became a bridge over a deep inky chasm. Annette heard water trickling down the rock walls. Nervously she edged out onto the bridge. It span about four feet wide. Their footsteps echoed faintly. The bridge ended and the pathway led upward. Towering jagged cavern walls enclosed them again on either side. Suddenly they gave way and the torchlight seemed to glare back in unusual brightness. Annette gasped. The flickering light made the walls sparkle like stars in the heavens. They were in a cavern of gold.

"It's beautiful!" Whispered Annette.

Eric said nothing. He put the torch in an iron holder that stood against a wall to his left. He watched Annette as she tiptoed further into the cavern and spun around marvelling at the glittering cavern.

"Now I understand," she said.

"We treated strangers with kindness and they tried to pay us back in death," replied Eric. "But none succeeded." His face grew grim. Annette shrank back. Eric's face quickly softened as he noticed her fear. His eyes glanced around and fell back on Annette. He stepped closer to her and took her hand. "Come."

They walked through the cavern. At various spots along the wall Annette saw pickaxes and shovels leaning against wooden wheelbarrows. Near a wall in the back of the cavern was a wooden door. "It leads to the dungeon," said Eric as he gestured toward the door. "Our prisoners come and work the mine. The gold we trade with the skarelings for supplies."

"Interesting," said Annette. "Can we go now? I'm getting cold."

"Then I will make you warm," Eric took her in his arms. Annette tried to push away but he was too strong. His right hand gripped her head and he forced a kiss upon his lips. She bit his lip and stomped down on the instep of his right foot. Eric yelled and released her. Annette turned and ran towards the door. It wasn't locked. She stepped through the doorway, slamming the door behind her and ran down a dark narrow passageway. Another door barred her path. This one was locked. She struggled with the handle, and pounded on the door.

"There's no place else to run. Why do you run from me? I will not hurt you," whispered Eric.

Annette turned, her back to the door. Eric limped towards her. He held a torch in his left hand. He reached out to grab her with his right hand. Annette screamed.

***

Malloy tucked the white cotton shirt into dark navy blue trousers, and buttoned them up. He bent over to pull on a pair of short, black, soft leather boots. The clean clothes had been brought in while they slept. He glanced at the bed. Freydis was still asleep, tired from their frantic lovemaking. Quietly, Malloy left the room. Once in the corridor he made his way back quickly to the dungeon.

Dirk sat by a table in the torture room. He was a young brawny dark-haired fellow. He yawned. Guard duty was a boring, tiring affair. Dirk couldn't understand why anyone had to guard the prisoners. Where would they go? They certainly were in no condition to escape. What he needed was a good cup of ale and a companion to pass the time with, preferably female. He envied Eric who was with the foreign woman. Dirk heard a soft scuffle of feet behind him. He turned around, wondering if Bjarne had come early to relieve him.

Malloy's fist crashed into Dirk's jaw. The young man went flying out of his chair and landed on his back. He sprung to his feet, but while he was in a half-crouch, Malloy lashed out with his foot. It caught Dirk full in the face. He fell back, cracking his head on the stone floor. Dazed, Dirk felt strong hands bind him with leather thongs. He struggled. Another fist hit the side of his head and he fell unconscious.

Malloy shook his hand. The kid had one tough skull. He found a piece of cloth and gagged the guard. He took the keys off the rack and walked into the cell corridor.

"Thank God!" cried Bouchard.

"Easy, we'll have you out in no time." Malloy peered into the cell next to Bouchard. "Colton, are you all right?"

"Yes," Colton groaned. He struggled to his feet. He stretched and pain shot down his back. "They gave me the lash." He grunted in pain. "Get me out of here."

Malloy had the key in Andre Bouchard's cell door when he heard Annette scream.

"My daughter!" yelled Bouchard.

"It's coming from the mine," said Wilkinson. "The door at the end of the corridor."

Malloy rushed to the door. It was locked. He tried a key. It didn't work. The next one did. He unlocked the door and slammed it open. Annette fell through the doorway. Her blouse was ripped. Malloy looked up to see Eric standing there in surprise. He stepped in quickly before Eric could recover and belted him a hard right to the stomach. Eric doubled over and Malloy clasped his hands together and brought them down hard at the base of Eric's skull. Eric hit the floor face first. He rolled over. His nose bled. His face was cut and scraped. The young Viking groaned and lay still on the ground. Malloy helped Annette to her feet. She clutched Malloy tightly around the waist. She sobbed. "He was showing me the mine. He'd been so polite this morning, then he attacked me."

Malloy glared down at the prone figure. "Looks like I'll have to teach him some manners."

At that moment a pack of guards broke into the corridor. They grabbed Malloy. Dirk was among them. His fist caught Malloy on the side of the face. Malloy's head rocked back.

"Enough." It was Queen Freydis. The guards parted for her. She surveyed her unconscious son and the condition of Annette's blouse. She turned to Malloy. "This is how you repay my hospitality?" Freydis was hurt and angry. She then turned to the guards and spoke in her Norse dialect, "Pick him up and take him to his room," ordered Freydis to two of the men.

Malloy struggled to free himself, but the guards held his arms tightly. He relaxed. There was no use getting angry now. It wouldn't help them. Freydis studied his expressionless face. "You were going to free your friends." she said.

"If you were in my position, you would do the same."

"I am not in your position. Perhaps I was wrong about you. You are no better than the others." She turned and stared at Annette. "You will be wed to my son. Bjarne, take her to the tower room." A young guard stepped forward. "If she tries to escape, kill her."

"What about him?" asked Dirk, thumbing towards Malloy.

"It seems he prefers the company of men to that of me. He can work in the mine with his friends. Perhaps a few days there will change your mind, yes?" She smiled, then turned sharply around and marched out of the dungeon.

Dirk looked at Malloy. "Eric is my comrade."

Malloy saw the punch coming and managed to roll with it. The fist just grazed his cheek. Another fist hit his stomach. Suddenly pain filled his head and he fell to the floor. He passed into unconsciousness as the real beating began.

Malloy was thrown into a cell across from Wilkinson. The room spun. His ribs and stomach ached. He tasted blood from a cut on his lip. He closed his eyes. The iron barred door clanged shut. The sound echoed in the dark corridor.

CHAPTER SEVENTEEN: WORKING THE MINE

Time lost its meaning in the dark cellblock. The prisoners were aroused and fed a quick breakfast of gruel, then marched down the corridor and through the stout wooden door that lead to the mine. The walked down stone corridors, few required any type of supporting beams. It seemed that the Vikings used the cavern's natural labyrinths. The Head guard, Bjarne, stopped along one passage. He gestured to one of the five guards. A young man stepped forward and passed out short handled pickaxes to Malloy, Colton and Wilkinson. He gave a woven basket to Bouchard.

"Now work you sons of dogs. Dig for your gold," he laughed.

"And don't even think about escape." Helmut, Reijo, watch them."

Two dark complexioned barrel chested men of medium height stepped forward. Helmut was an older man with a patch over one eye and a scar down his left cheek. A leather whip was rolled and hung off a thong on his belt. Reijo was a younger man with silver white hair and gray eyes. A short broadsword hung from a sheath around his waist.

"To work!" roared Helmut. He snapped his whip.

"Don't cross that bugger," warned Wilkinson. "He's a nasty bastard."

"That is right," laughed Helmut. He snapped the whip over Colton's head.

Henry cringed at the sound and recovered, giving Helmut a nasty glare. He selected a spot on the wall and swung the axe. Chips of quartz and limestone exploded. Henry averted his head in time to be spared being blinded by the flying chips.

With fury, Malloy attacked a section of rock wall. Chips flew. Some cut his face. His anger soon subsided and he slowed down to a steady pace, occasionally sneaking glances at the guards. He wasn't going to be as rash as to try to escape immediately; but he wanted to study their movements and habits. Once he knew his enemy, he'd spot the weak point that would give him the advantage.

Henry Bouchard examined the bits of rock and selected those fragments that contained any gold.

Wilkinson worked at a slow but steady pace.

How long they worked they didn't know. Colton was the first to put down his axe. His rag of a shirt was drenched in sweat. He turned to Helmut. "Can I have some water?"

Helmut laughed and spit on the stone floor. "You've barely begun. I will tell you when to rest and when to drink," said Helmut.

Colton held his tongue. He eyed the whip in Helmut's fist. His back still sore from the lashing he'd received the day before. He's another one. Slowly Henry turned around and picked up the pickaxe. He eyed a spot on the cavern wall and swung the axe into it. Chips sparked and flew.

When they finished that day there was little talk. They were herded back to the dungeon cellblock. That night they ate silently and went to sleep. Too soon, the cycle would repeat itself.

The backbreaking work continued. Days blurred together. Each day Malloy noticed that the breaks were less frequent, as were water and food. Nobody talked. Malloy kept an eye on the guards. The younger guards changed shifts, but Helmut was always present. He was a man who seemed to take pleasure in commanding others, even bullying and teasing his own people. Yet, despite his cruelty, they seemed to respect him. Malloy questioned Reijo one evening about Helmut but learned little other than that the man was a good warrior and hunter. He'd gotten the scar in a fight with a grizzly. The bear's hide was now a rug in the man's hut.

"Break!" yelled Reijo.

The men dropped their tools. Malloy's white shirt was torn at the sleeves and gray from dust and sweat. Dust covered Wilkinson and Colton. Malloy watched as Reijo came around with a wooden bucket of water and a ladle. Each man received one spoonful.

"Drink slowly," reminded Henry Bouchard. "Rinse the dust out of your mouth."

Malloy sipped the water. It was ice cold. He spit out the second mouthful and ran his tongue around the inside of his mouth. He sipped some more. Suddenly he stopped. Malloy gazed at his fellow prisoners. He looked at Wilkinson, then Colton. Both were leaning against the wall. Torchlight flickering from behind cast their shadows along one wall. Malloy stared at the profile, and then realized that there was a family resemblance. Father and son? He thought about what the stories said about Wilkinson, and remembered the few details that Colton had mentioned about growing up in San Francisco. It was possible. Yet Colton had shown no recognition when he had seen Wilkinson. Of course the man had left when Henry was quite young. Undoubtedly Henry harbored some resentment. But surely Henry knew. Given his temperament Malloy wondered what sort of revenge Henry planned for his father. He doubted Henry had any good intentions. Malloy knew that such feelings could sabotage any escape he might plan as well. He'd have to watch their interaction more closely.

Malloy finished his drink. Reijo took the bucket over to Henry Bouchard.

"The rest of you back to work!" yelled Helmut as he snapped his whip over their heads.

Work progressed slowly. They worked different portions of the mine every day. No one except George knew how much gold they'd actually found. Occasionally Helmut would go and examine the basket. When the basket was full Reijo took it away and brought another one.

"Break!" roared Helmut.

The men dropped their pickaxes and collapsed on the floor. Reijo passed out wooden bowls. Another guard came with a bucket of stew and a loaf of bread. Each man received two ladles full and a chunk of bread. At least thought Malloy they weren't being starved.

Wilkinson wolfed his food down. Malloy watched Colton staring at his father. There was pure hate in his eyes.

"What happened with you and the McLeod's?" asked Malloy.

Wilkinson burped. " 'Scuse me. We panned up the Flat. We noticed that the further west we went, the more tracings we found. Willie got the idea to head towards the mountains, rather than piss around placer mining. We found this place by accident. We actually came across it by coming round the other side. Found us nuggets big as a man's fist. Course we didn't know that there was more than one entrance to the place. Anyway we were in the middle of working when a few of these fellows came upon us. They were armed with bows, arrows, swords, spears, and these shiny metal disks that were sharpened around the edge. They come a whooping and a hollering at us. Naturally we shot them and ran like hell. I got caught right before we were to set off down the river. Got an arrow through my left arm, and fell out of the boat. Willie and Frank didn't wait around and I didn't blame them. But I know they didn't make it. Their heads were brought back on spears."

"They got as far as the second canyon," said Malloy. "Charlie led a search party. I was part of it. Why they cut the heads off?"

"I don't quite know. They got some silly pagan beliefs mixed in with their Christian teaching. There's a room here that's full of heads. Has an altar in it too."

"We saw it when we were brought here. Andre is there," whispered George Bouchard.

Colton ate in silence, but Malloy could tell he was taking it all in.

"Know anything about the fires?" He then told them about Phil Power's cabin.

"These Vikings are barbarians. They're always burning something. Don't be fooled by their so-called manners," said Wilkinson. "They burned the remainder of Andre. They shoved this strange brew down his throat and his body burned from the inside out. We were forced to watch. I hear sometimes they dress the victim again in their own clothes after, to scare their enemies."

Malloy glanced at George. Tears welled in the man's eyes.

"Enough talk. Back to work," ordered Helmut. He bent over and knocked the bowl out of Wilkinson's hand. His eyes flashed quickly at Malloy.

Malloy sat quietly. He wasn't about to make anything out of Helmut's behavior yet. Malloy knew the man was still trying to size them up. He wasn't about to be goaded. When the time came, it would be on Malloy's terms.

A sharp stab of pain greeted Henry Colton in the morning. Colton's eyes fluttered open and he rolled over. "Ugh!" cried Colton. He curled into a foetal position and looked up. Helmut stood over him. In his right hand was a stout wooden staff.

"Get up you lazy dog. Time for you to work in the mine."

Colton groaned and got to his hands and knees. He took a deep breath. He glanced at Helmut. The guard was raising his staff again.

"I'm getting up," coughed Colton. Slowly he rose to his feet. Outside the cell, Malloy, Henry and Wilkinson were lined up. Dirk and Reijo guarded them. "Don't I get breakfast?"

"You slept through it." Helmut pointed with the staff to a bowl in the corner.

Colton took two steps towards the bowl of cold porridge. Helmut tipped it with the staff. The bowl flipped over, spilling its contents on the floor.

"Lick it up if you like," he laughed.

"You sonofabitch," cursed Colton.

Helmut cocked his head and regarded Colton a moment. "You want to kill me don't you?"

Colton didn't reply, but anger blazed in his eyes.

"Go ahead. Take a swing," goaded Helmut.

"Don't be a fool Colton," warned Malloy.

"Shut up!" yelled back Helmut. His eyes remained on Colton. "Go ahead you spineless dog."

Colton swung a fast right at Helmut's jaw. The Viking sidestepped the blow and brought the staff swiftly into Colton's stomach. The younger man buckled forward and fell to his knees. "Feel better. Get up. We go. "Helmut looked at the others. "At least he has spirit." His eyes met Malloy's. Not yet you bastard thought Malloy.

Again they were marched to a different spot in the mine. Malloy could hear water dripping faintly in the darkness. Two torches were placed in holders along one wall. Malloy looked up at the glittering cavern. Henry Colton gasped in awe. Never had he seen so much raw unmined gold.

"Now you see why men died to find this," said Wilkinson.

"The dream," whispered George Bouchard.

Under the light, Malloy could see that the area had been worked before. Dirk gave pickaxes to Malloy and Wilkinson and a shovel to Colton. Like before, George Bouchard sat with a woven basket to examine and sort the gold.

Despite the dampness of the cavern, it didn't take long for the men to work up a sweat. Time had no meaning. It seemed longer though then the day before when Helmut finally told them to rest.

This time there was no water for their break. But at least they could sit down. It was cool in the cave when they weren't working. Malloy shivered. This was a good way to get sick. They wouldn't last long. It was a miracle that Wilkinson and Bouchard had survived as long as they had. He glanced over at Colton. Malloy noticed the trembling of Colton's arms. The young man was tired.

"Okay you lazy women. Back to work." growled Helmut. He thudded the ground with his wooden staff.

Slowly Malloy got up and stretched. He helped Wilkinson to his feet.

"Thank you. Don't know what's up with the bugger today," he whispered.

"Quiet!" ordered Helmut. "Save your strength for working, not talking."

He walked over to Colton. "What's with you? Get up." He tapped Henry on the shoulder with his staff.

Colton winced. He got to his knees. "Okay. I'm getting up!" With a roar Colton butted Helmut in the groin with his head.

The Viking bellowed and bent over. He clutched his balls with his left hand. Colton lashed out with his fists and hit Helmut in his stomach and face. The Viking staggered back still clutching the staff with his right hand. He hit the cave wall. Helmut shook his head and roared. He took a step toward Colton and swung with the staff. Colton leaped aside. He bent over and picked up a nugget from the basket. He hurled it at Helmut. It struck Helmut a glancing blow on the left shoulder.

"Now we'll see what you're made of," hissed Helmut, a dark grin spreading across his face. He threw the staff aside and released the whip. He lashed out at Colton. The whip snaked around Henry's right arm. Henry winced at the pain, but didn't give into it. He grabbed the whip with his left hand and pulled. Helmut slid a step or two then stopped. He laughed.

Colton unwound the whip from his right arm. His forearm bled from a gash. Helmut pulled the whip back. He lashed out again. Colton dove under it and tackled Helmut. Both men rolled on the ground as they struggled.

Malloy watched Dirk. So far, the young guard's attention had not been drawn toward the fight. He had kept his eyes on the other prisoners.

Helmut sat astride Henry. His strong hands gripped around Henry's neck. Colton tried to pull one of the hands away. He was gasping for breath. Helmut threw his head back and laughed.

Dirk smiled and glanced at the older man. It was all Malloy needed. He leaped across the narrow corridor. Malloy's shadow crossed Dirk's periphery vision. Dirk's head snapped up. He grasped at the sword in its sheath. Too late! Malloy flung himself on the guard. Dirk crashed against the wall. Malloy's massive fist crashed into his stomach. Dirk buckled. Hands clasped, Malloy brought them down on the young Viking's neck. Dirk groaned and hit the floor face first. Malloy picked up Helmut's staff.

"Hey, old man!" he yelled at Helmut.

"What?" Helmut looked up.

Malloy smashed the staff into Helmut's face. Helmut wailed. The Viking released his grip on Colton. His hands flew to his face. Blood ran down from his smashed nose and teeth. He staggered to his feet. Malloy hit Helmut in the stomach with the end of the staff. The Viking fell to his knees and rolled over Colton.

Wilkinson ran to Colton and helped him to his feet.

Helmut coughed. "Damn you," he growled at Malloy.

Malloy let Helmut regain his stance, and then smacked him in the face again with the staff. Helmut staggered back against the wall. Malloy threw away the staff. He smashed his left fist into Helmut's solar plexus and his right fist cracked Helmut's jaw. The Viking slid to a heap on the floor.

Malloy retrieved the short broadsword and the whip. He gave the staff to Bouchard.

"Let's go gentlemen," he said.

"It's a lost cause friend, though we appreciate it," said Wilkinson.

"They will extract their revenge for this." He gestured at the prone bodies.

"Not if we get our weapons," gasped Colton.

"It will give us an advantage," said Malloy. Using Helmut's whip, he bound the two guards. "Let's go."

Malloy grabbed a torch from its holder and led the men out of the cavern.

CHAPTER EIGHTEEN: ANNETTE'S FATE

Almost two weeks had passed since Malloy had rescued Annette from Eric's attack. She had not seen the Viking prince during that time. Her days were mostly spent alone in the tower room. To pass the time, Annette observed from the turret windows what she could of village life. In the morning the few old women gossiped as they walked down to the lake to wash clothes; in the afternoon they returned to the river to bring back water. Sometimes, armed with small baskets, they would head into the forest, to what Annette assumed was a search for herbs or berries. The younger women went out in groups every day to tend fields, while the men, armed with bows, arrows or fishing poles, went out to hunt and fish. She had heard that some of the natives ventured out into civilization to trade for items that the people couldn't supply themselves. Annette also knew there was a pub in the village where the men congregated in the evening swilling back tankards of homemade brew. Life in the idyllic village of Asgard consisted of routine and boredom. Annette realized too that life in Fort Simpson or Fort Laird was similar. And, she realized that she longed to return to civilization, as she knew it with theaters and restaurants, and museums and intellectual conversation.

One morning after delivering breakfast, Hubert took pity on her and sneaked her down to the library. The library consisted of a wood panelled room with a row of shelves along one wall containing various scrolls and ancient texts. A long table and four chairs were placed in the middle of the room. Annette surveyed the shelves. Most of the scrolls were written on parchment using runes, and the texts in French. The books proved mostly to be theological, and outdated scientific and agricultural subject matter. There was also a dictionary, a tattered copy of the King James Bible, and school primers in French and English. Annette did find a few samples of literature: Les Miserables by Victor Hugo, The Three Musketeers by Alexander Dumas, and a collection of stories by Washington Irving. Annette took the book by Washington Irving.

Upon returning to her room, Annette curled up on her bed and began to read. Sometime later there was a knock on her door. She hid the book under her pillow. Queen Freydis entered. She looked tired Annette noticed.

"I have come to discuss your wedding," she announced.

"Wedding?" Annette sat up on the bed.

"To Eric. He has recovered, and I talked to him about his behavior. Now we must talk, as a mother to her daughter-in-law." The Queen sat down in a chair across from the bed. "He is a young man who acts on rather crude emotions. But you too must learn your place. He has much to offer."

"I am not in love with your son, nor could I be. He doesn't have the qualities I seek in a man," said Annette.

"And what qualities are those? He is brave, strong, a little slow, but not stupid."

"He is egotistical, crude and hard. I've really yet to see a gentle, kind side to his nature," replied Annette.

"You prefer the old man Malloy? He will be dead long before your beauty fades," sneered Freydis," And the other one, the man Henry Colton, is a braggart and a swine. He cares not for you," said Freydis. "My son Eric is better than he."

"Surely there are women in the village," replied Annette.

"Yes, but few. We have more men then women. Those women service many men. The skraelings are not like us. And Eric is a prince. He needs an educated, refine woman. No, you are the one for him."

"Well, I don't love him."

"That matters not." Freydis waved a hand heedlessly. "Bare him fine sons. He has much to do. You don't have to share all your time with him." The Queen rose. "I'm glad we had this talk. Preparations are under way. The wedding will take place in two days." She walked to the door and paused. "Do not fret my dear. Things could be much worse. And don't forget your friends." With that subtle threat Freydis left the room. The door clicked shut behind her.

Tears welled in Annette's eyes, but she held them back. She had to escape and free her father and the others.

Time slipped away like grains of sand washed out by ocean waves. Annette paced her room. Under guard she was allowed to stroll in the garden. Looking up she studied her tower room. The bars on the window and the height removed any thoughts of escape from that route. It would have to be from the inside, and therein lay the greater risk.

Mary visited her later that afternoon.

"You are feeling sad." she commented. "I do not blame you. Prince Eric is a cruel and rude man. But there is nothing you can do about it. Come with me, I will help you relax."

Mary led Annette down the turret stairs and into the main corridor. Going through another door they descended stone steps leading to a wooden door. Annette noticed that the air was now hot and humid, not cool like she had expected.

"There is natural hot springs under the palace. The sea people have made a sweathouse here; as well there is a hot pool. You will find it relaxing."

Mary opened the door. The heat almost made Annette faint. Through a thin steam haze Annette found that the chamber contained two rooms. One was a steam room with wooden benches. The other was a natural rock chamber with a pool of steaming water.

"Undress and enjoy. I will bring you towels," said Mary.

Annette stripped and stepped into the pool. The water was hot, but not scalding. She swam slowly and found a spot where she could prop her head against a rocky ledge and float. Her muscles relaxed as she felt the gentle rhythm of the current swirl around her. But her mind remained active as she planned her escape.

When Annette returned to her room late that afternoon she lay out trousers, boots, a shirt and jacket and hid them under her bed. Then she hunted around for a weapon. The chair and table were too heavy for her to wield. She went to the clothes cupboard and pulled out the wooden bar from which the clothes were hung. It was a solid piece of wood. Annette made several practice swings. It would have to do until she could lay her hands on something deadlier.

That evening she heard heavy footsteps on the stairwell. She didn't recognize as being either Hubert's or Mary's. Her heart started beating. Suppose it was Eric? Or one of the other guards? Her hands were shaking as she picked up the wooden rod and hid behind the door. She heard the key turn in the lock. The door opened slowly. Annette braced herself, ready to swing the club down on the person as soon as they entered the room.

CHAPTER NINETEEN: ESCAPE

Falstaff sat at the table guarding the weapons room located off the entrance to the dungeon. He was a hulking brown-haired young man with a heavy beard. Falstaff closed his eyes. It seemed silly to guard a room when the only prisoners were slaving away in the mine. He'd much rather have been hunting or wenching. But Bjarne had been quite insistent. After all who would steal them? The foreigner's weapons were powerful, but more complex. He much preferred to trust his bow and sword than any miniature boom cannon. Falstaff yawned and stretched his arms. Guard duty was a boring lot.

Malloy and Colton sneaked quietly through the rear door leading to the prison corridor. They crept down and Malloy peered through the doorway into the main torture chamber. He saw Falstaff, turned and whispered to Colton, "They left one guard. Let me go first. Be ready to rush in when I call."

"Go ahead," nodded Colton. Behind him he heard George and Wilkinson shuffling closer.

Malloy rushed forward on the balls of his feet. A stone crunched under his step. The guard turned and saw him. He began to stand, drawing his sword, but Malloy was upon him. Two swift blows brought the young guard to his knees. Malloy picked up the chair and swung it down on Falstaff's head. The guard lay still.

"Come on," Malloy called as he bent over and retrieved the keys from the guard's pocket. He opened the door. Light poured into the darkened room and Malloy could see a variety of weapons stacked against the walls and piled on the floor. There were a number of rifles and pistols of varying ages. Malloy, with Colton behind him, entered the room and began rummaging for his weapons. Malloy noticed that a few of the rifles were flintlocks, real museum pieces he reflected. Next to the flintlocks were some small leather pouches. Inside were pieces of flint. Malloy pocketed a couple of the pouches. The stones would come in handy for lighting torches. He also found his pack, still containing supplies and a smaller leather knapsack with a shirt, matches, and hand-axe in it. He gave the knapsack to Colton.

While looking through the assortment of guns, knives and swords, Colton found a small wooden box. Opening it, he discovered it contained several sticks of dynamite. Glancing around to make sure no one was looking, he stuck two sticks inside the knapsack. When the time came, he intended to pay his father and Malloy back for the indignities they had inflicted upon him.

"Over here," called Malloy. He'd found his weapons. "Here, these might suit you." He handed Colton a Winchester and an old Colt revolver.

"This feels better." Malloy checked the bolt action of his rifle.

"I'll say." Colton shoved the old Colt revolver through his belt and picked up an old Winchester repeater.

"Let me check that," said Malloy. Colton handed him the rifle. Malloy checked the lever action and barrel. "It's okay. See if you can find some shells for it."

Colton looked around and found a small box of shells. He showed the box to Malloy. "These the right kind?"

"Yep," replied Malloy quickly examining the box. Wilkinson poked his head in. "We should hurry. Bjarne does rounds to check on the guards."

"Henry, help Wilkinson to bring that guard in here. We'll tie him up. Bjarne probably won't check the room. He'll think the kid deserted his post," said Malloy.

"Right," nodded Henry. "Good idea." He went out and gave Wilkinson a hand. Together they dragged the unconscious guard inside.

Malloy gave a last look and found a Colt .45 automatic and another rifle which he each gave to Bouchard and Wilkinson.

A few minutes later Malloy and the others re-entered the mine. Malloy locked the door behind them. "This should help slow anyone down trying to enter from this way. Okay Wilkinson, where do we go from here?"

Wilkinson edged his way around to the front of the group. "This way. We'll go out through the entrance George and I used originally. It'll be easier entering the palace from the outside then trying to go through the throne room."

"He's right," said Bouchard. "And you must rescue my Annette."

"Don't worry, we'll get her back," promised Malloy.

They set out single file down the mine corridor. Torch in hand, Wilkinson led, followed by Colton, Bouchard and Malloy. The ground was hard and dusty beneath their feet.

"We've been together over a week, and no word of greeting for your father Henry?" whispered Wilkinson.

Henry's eyes barely flickered in the shadowy light. "What did you expect me to say? You left us."

"Do you want to know why?" asked Wilkinson.

"The gold."

"Yes, the gold, but that wasn't the only reason. I was being kept. I didn't like it. Every chance your mother got, she rubbed her wealth in my nose," said Wilkinson. There was a hard edge to his voice.

"You married her for her money didn't you?"

"Partially. Back then I did have some money of my own from the first trip here and a few investments. Truth is, your grandfather paid me to marry her. He got tired of hearing how no one was good enough for her and didn't want a spinster for a daughter. He was getting on and he wanted a male heir. I gave them what they wanted. Finally."

"And when I was born you left," spat Henry. "I hate you for that. Grandfather died. His inheritance went to Mother. Do you know what it's like growing up in a house full of women?"

"I didn't leave because of you. I left because I couldn't take it anymore. All the nagging, the bragging. I knew that if I were ever to win your mother's approval, I'd have to be as rich as she. Then, there would be no hold." Wilkinson took a deep breath. "How did you find me?" asked Wilkinson.

"I chanced to meet Annette Bouchard through a friend. I gained her confidence. She told me about her father's expedition and the fact that you were with them. It was a lucky break. All my other means of tracking you had lead to naught."

"And now that you've found me?" Wilkinson glanced back at his son. He saw the mask of hate revealed by the flickering torchlight.

"Quite dawdling," complained George Bouchard.

Wilkinson turned his attention to the task at hand. They walked a bit further, and then stopped. Wilkinson held the torch out in front of him.

"We've got to cross a stone bridge. It's quite slippery. I suggest we crawl across on our hands and knees. It's a long drop if anyone falls."

Bending onto all fours, Wilkinson slowly crawled out onto the bridge. The bridge was barely a foot wide and spanned for at least one hundred feet across a deep crevice. Below, Colton could hear water running.

"There's a river below," he said.

"Yes, it runs underground to the lake," replied his father.

Malloy shouted from behind, "Hurry up! We've got company coming."

A series of low yells echoed through the cavern.

"Looks like they found out we've gone," commented George Bouchard. "I suggest we speed our crossing."

Wilkinson and Henry began crawling faster. Suddenly Wilkinson's hand slipped. He fell forward and started sliding off. Henry clutched his other arm. "Easy. I got you."

"Thanks son." Wilkinson felt his heart pounding. He turned briefly and looked at his son. Henry's face remained expressionless. Wilkinson turned and began crawling again. Henry followed closely behind him.

They heard Malloy's revolver fire. It thundered in their ears. A spear sailed over there heads and down into the chasm.

"Almost there," sighed Wilkinson. He saw the ledge of the canyon wall. A path leads along it and around into a web of caverns. Through one of them was the entrance to the outside.

Despite his handicap, George Bouchard moved with speed and coordination. In the dim torchlight he could see his partner climb onto the ledge. Wilkinson was bending over to help Henry off the bridge. He had a torch in his left hand while he offered his right to the young man. And then, George Bouchard screamed.

"NO!"

An arrow sailed over Henry's head and thrust into Wilkinson's middle, pinning him to the wall. A wail of pain reverberated in the cavern and died with Wilkinson's last breath. The torch sailed out of his hand and the cave plunged into darkness.

Bracing his pistol arm on the bridge, Malloy aimed and fired twice towards the flickering torchlight behind him. He heard a yell and saw a dark shape dive off the bridge into the blackness. That should discourage them for a little while he thought. Quickly he turned and clambered across. Colton was helping George Bouchard up.

Malloy stood up and leaning against the canyon wall, fired again down the bridge's path. In the brief light of gunfire, Colton saw a figure crawling across the bridge. He unslung the rifle from his back and aimed low. He heard a grunt.

"Not bad. Think you winged him," said Malloy. Turning to Bouchard,

"Which way?"

Bouchard, hobbling on one foot and a crude crutch, he hugged the wall, and climbed around his dead companion. "This way. Be careful. The path will widen out shortly."

They travelled slowly in the darkness. Soon the narrow path widened, and from the air on his face, Malloy knew they were once again in a large cavern.

"Keep to your right. I suggest we try and hold on to one another," said Bouchard.

"Come on Henry, grab a side," said Malloy. With a man on either side supporting him, George Bouchard led them.

"I don't hear anything," whispered Henry.

"That doesn't mean they aren't behind us. They're just quieter," cautioned Malloy.

They continued on for a few minutes, and then Bouchard squeezed Malloy's hand to signal that they had to stop.

"What's wrong?" whispered Malloy.

"I don't know. I'm not feeling any wind from outside. I may have taken a wrong turn. I need light."

"Great!" muttered Colton. He stood quietly, listening. He couldn't hear any footsteps behind them.

Suddenly there was a whoosh by Malloy's right. He heard the arrow bounce off the cave wall.

"They're here! Down!" Malloy sprawled on the cavern floor and unslung the rifle. He jacked a shell into the chamber.

Suddenly the cavern was filled with war whoops and a blaze with torchlight as a dozen Vikings rushed towards them. Malloy aimed his rifle and fired. Thunder and lightning of gunfire flashed and shook the cavern. George Bouchard, a fierce expression of hatred on his face, crouched behind a rock; and, using the old Colt revolver Colton had given him, he fired at the charging hoard. Colton, like Malloy, was sprawled on the floor near a mound of boulders. He blasted their attackers. Dead bodies lay sprawled on the ground, several had fallen off the stone bridge and into the abyss. But these were tough men, even those wounded pressed forward and continued fighting.

Malloy fired at one Viking as the man threw a hatchet. He staggered and roared as blood spurted from his chest. The hatchet flew across the room and split George Bouchard's head like a hammer hitting a ripe melon. Bouchard fell back and lay still. Damn! Malloy aimed carefully and fired until his rifle was empty, then he took his revolver and fired into the few remaining attackers.

Colton rested behind a boulder as he crammed fresh bullets into the Winchester. His heart was pounding and his head ringing from the resounding echoes of the gunfire. His hands shook. Anger poured through his veins. The Vikings had denied him his vengeance. He had wanted to shove his father into the chasm at the bridge, but that would've been a swift retribution. And now, his father was dead by another's hand. George Bouchard's right eye stared at him. Blood spread out like a red flowing lake beneath the split skull. Henry wriggled over to Bouchard. As he reached out to close Bouchard's eye, he noticed a pouch that spilled out of his shirt. Colton took the pouch and opened it. It was filled with gold nuggets. The sonofabitch had managed to steal some of the gold they had mined. Colton took the pouch and put it in his knapsack. At least he'd get reimbursed for some of his troubles. Colton turned and fired again.

"Hold it Henry. They're all dead!" yelled Malloy.

Not yet thought Henry, you're still alive.

CHAPTER TWENTY: A MOTHER'S FURY

Annette heard the key turn in the lock. The door opened slowly. She braced herself, ready to swing the club down on the person as soon as they entered the room. A shadow crossed the floor. Annette looked at it, and then lifted her head. It was Eric.

"Annette, it is I. I've come for you." Eric stopped. "Annette?"

He was two-thirds into the room when she crashed the club down on the back of his skull. Eric fell to floor dazed but not unconscious. He shook his head and turned up to see Annette standing over him, the club at her side. He smiled wickedly, slowly picking himself up. He was in a crouch when Annette smashed her booted foot into his groin. Eric bellowed and sank to his knees. Annette brought the club up and smacked his head. The club broke. She took the remaining piece in her hands and whacked him in face. Eric hollered and fell back in agony. Blood spurted from his nose and poured onto the floor in a widening river as he rolled on the floor in pain. Annette tried to step over him. He grabbed her ankle and hauled her down. He climbed on top of her, ignoring the flailing fists and clawing.

"Now I teach you how to be a Viking wife," he growled. Pinning her right hand with his left, he swatted her with the open palm of his right hand. Pain numbed Annette's face and she tasted blood from a cut on her lip. Eric straddled her; blood from his nose ran down his face and fell like raindrops on her shirt. He wiped his nose with the back of his hand, then reached down ripped her shirt open. Annette tried to twist out from under him. He squeezed her left breast with his right hand. His left hand still pinned her right to the floor. He bent over to suck her breasts. She clawed his face. Eric sat back up and wiped his right cheek. His eyes blazed. He grinned.

"You still have spirit," he panted. "Good, it will be a challenge to break it. And when I do, you will be mine."

He smacked at her again with an open palm; She partially blocked the blow with her free hand. Eric pinned the hand and bent over. He crushed his lips to hers. Annette struggled twisting and turning her head from his wet lips. She wiggled her left hand free. Glancing down she saw the dagger in the sheath on his belt. She stretched her fingers desperately attempting to grasp it and he continued to shower her with kisses and feel her breasts.

Eric swatted her hand away then began fumbling with the belt to her pants. Annette reached again. With her forefinger she felt the hilt of the knife. Her two middle fingers managed to move it up from the sheath. Eric unbuttoned her pants. His hand groped inside. Annette gasped and tried to squirm away. He undid his belt. Annette felt his hot breath on her neck as he kissed her. She grasped the hilt and pulled the knife out. Turning it she thrust it up to the hilt into Eric's side.

He screamed and reared up. In alarm he grasped for the knife. His eyes were wide with panic. His hands clasped the hilt over hers; but the knife was in deep and he didn't have the leverage he needed. Annette now grasped the hilt with both hands pulled it towards her, widening the cut. Eric let out a stifled wail. Blood poured out like water from a gushing dam. Annette released her hold on the knife. Eric rolled off her and curled up on the floor. He groaned.

Annette scampered out from under him. She lay panting in a corner. She was covered in blood. Hastily she buttoned her sodden stained pants, and then using the wall for support, she crawled up to a standing position. Frantically she looked around for another weapon, eyed the chair, picked it up and smashed it over him. Annette staggered back and leaned against the wall. She wiped the sweat from her brow and took a deep breath. She was trembling.

Eric lay still. He was barely breathing. Annette shut the door and waited; but she heard no footsteps. The sound hadn't carried. The tower room was far enough from the rest of the quarters.

Annette went to the closet and changed her clothes, flinging the bloody torn remnants in disgust on the floor. Cautiously she approached the dying prince and gingerly tried to pull the knife out. Eric grunted semi-consciously. Annette felt she was going to be sick. But she needed a weapon. Steeling herself, she pressed her foot on his body, bent over to gain better leverage and yanked the knife out. The motion flung her against the bed. The river of blood increased. There was a large pool underneath Eric. Splatters of blood made puddles on the floor. Annette wiped the knife on the bedspread and thrust it through her belt. She gathered her supplies. The key was in the door. she shut and locked the door behind her, and swiftly walked downstairs.

Annette waited at the bottom of the stairs, peering cautiously out into the corridor. There were no guards about. Where to go next was the problem. She wanted to free her father and the others, but knew attempting to sneak into the dungeon now was impossible. Besides it was still afternoon. They'd be working in the mines. Annette knew she'd have to wait until evening. Until then she had to find a hiding place. All hell would break loose when they discovered Eric's body. A search would be made of the palace and the grounds, and most likely the village. Therefore the only place they probably wouldn't search is the mine and the area immediately outside the community. There wouldn't be time and Annette doubted they'd try searching for her at night. After all she was a woman, and less likely to be comfortable out in the bush. They'd also reason that she'd want to stay close to rescue her father and friends. And they'd be right. So where would that leave her?

Suddenly she heard a trampling of feet. She withdrew into the stairwell and shut the door. Annette heard voices. She picked out the words prisoners and dungeon. Something was going on. Perhaps Malloy and the others were making a break. If so, she needed to find them. She knew they'd come for her. But she couldn't remain here. The guard's footsteps retreated down the hall. Annette peeked out. The corridor was deserted. She stepped into it and headed for the main hall.

***

In the throne room Queen Freydis heard about the prisoners' revolt.

"They are armed and seek escape through the mine," reported Bjarne.

"Send in some guards after them. And send another squad to guard the mountain exit."

"I have already done so," said Bjarne.

"Good. We will take them. I want them alive, if possible. Then we will burn them at the stake." The Queen sighed angrily. "They are more trouble then they are worth."

"What about the woman?" he asked.

"Eric is taking her for a wife. By the way have you seen him?"

"I believe he was going to the woman's room M'lady," replied Bjarne.

Queen Freydis shook her head. Wouldn't that boy learn? Still, he was full of lust, and the girl, Annette, had to learn to please a Viking man. No doubt she had some experience. Queen Freydis stood up. Perhaps I should, but no she thought, there were more important tasks, the prisoners' escape being one. The girl would have to fend for herself. Freydis resumed her seat on the throne.

"Well, what are you standing here for Bjarne?" she snapped. "Go. Recapture the prisoners. Report to me when you have done so." Bjarne bowed, turned sharply on his heel and strode out of the hall. The two guards who remained in the throne room with the Queen eyed each other cautiously. Had it been up to either of them, they would've gladly followed Bjarne to battle, since there were so few these days.

Queen Freydis tapped her finger on the armrest. She felt impatient and upset. Her son was a nagging concern. Eric was no monarch. Despite what Freydis felt had been good teachers and counsellors, Eric was a failure. He didn't care about people. He wasn't overly intelligent, and basically Freydis had to admit, he thought with his manhood, not his head. She worried about her people. Times were changing. The outside world was encroaching on them with all its machines and men. The community would not be isolated for much longer, and then what?

Her worry turned to anger as Fredyis' thoughts turned to Malloy. Here was a man, an intelligent, strong man with leadership qualities her people needed. Here was someone that brought the fire to Freydis' heart for the first time in many years. A man who could satisfy her desires, and he scorned her for a woman old enough to be his daughter. How dare he reject her! Fredyis' right hand curled into a fist and smacked the armrest.

Shortly the restlessness grew within her, and she could no longer contain it. Freydis stood up and stepped down from the dais. "I go to see the girl prisoner. Remain here and keep an eye on the entrance to the dungeon in case the prisoners try to escape this way. Don't kill them if possible. I want them alive for the ceremony."
At this the guards smiled. "Yes, M'lady." Perhaps there would be excitement and entertainment after all. Beheadings were always something to look forward too.

Freydis marched out of the throne room and through the great hall.

Underneath a table in the shadows, in terror, Annette held her breath as the Queen's figure passed her. As soon as the Queen had left the great hall, Annette slipped out. She had to find a hiding place. Going through another doorway she found herself in a short anti-chamber. Before her was a set of ornately carved double doors. The doors' carvings were a mixture of animals such as Moose and deer and strange gargoyles and tall shaggy creatures. In the center of each door was an elongated cross. The imagery confused Annette, but she had little time to ponder. She opened one of the doors and entered.

Freydis went down the short hallway and opened the door to the stairwell leading to the tower room. Swiftly she mounted the stairs. Upon reaching the tower room door, she discovered it locked. She pounded on the door with her fist. "Annette? Eric!" She put her ear to the door but heard nothing. She looked around in dim, small corridor but the key was nowhere in sight. Her foot slipped. Freydis caught herself and looked down. A dark puddle was seeping from under the door. She bent down and put a finger in it. As she brought it to her, she saw that it was blood.

"Oh no," she moaned, "NO! HUBERT! MARY! GUARDS!" Freydis beat on the door with her fists. "Open up! Annette!"

Time stood still. Suddenly Freydis was aware of the sound of shuffling feet on the stairwell. "HURRY!"

"Coming your Highness," called up Hubert.

***

Annette fumbled in the darkness and found a torch in a wall brace. From her experience and exploration of the palace she knew that a holder of wooden matches lay on a wooden shelf on a nearby wall. She felt for it and found it. Striking a match, she reached up and lit the torch. The room she was in had pews. In the front on a small dais was some sort of altar. Annette concluded that this must be the chapel; and yet it was a dark gloomy sort of place. There were no windows. Shadows danced along the walls from the flickering torchlight. Annette stared at the walls. She choked as her eyes grew in horror. There on small hooks mounted on the walls were human heads, perfectly preserved. The eyes of the victims glittered in the torchlight and stared at her in horror and remorse. Annette screamed and fainted.

***

Hubert barely had a foot on the landing when Queen Freydis grabbed his arm and pulled him up. "Hurry, open the door."

Hubert reached into his jacket and pulled out a set of iron keys. "One moment Madam." He fumbled with the keys. Freydis grabbed them and jammed one of them into the lock. There was a click. She shoved the door open and almost tripped over Eric's body.

The Queen stood transfixed in horror. She stiffly and slowly knelt down and cradled Eric's head and torso in her arms. Blood stained her royal white gown. She stared at the lifeless face of her son. Tears welled in her eyes and streamed down her face. She looked up into the shocked, pale face of Hubert. She moaned. The moan grew into a wail that resounded off the walls.

CHAPTER TWENTY-ONE: ASGARD IN FLAMES

The dim light at the edge of the tunnel attracted Malloy and Colton like moths to a flame.

"I think we're gonna be home free Henry," said Malloy. "If the troops have forgotten about this exit."

"Perhaps, but don't forget, they've explored the cavern thoroughly. I'm sure they know about it," replied Malloy.

The light grew brighter.

"I see the opening," said Colton.

"Easy." Malloy stopped. "Let's load up. How's your ammo?"

"Still have half a box of shells for the Winchester, and I retrieved the pistol from George. Y'know, Annette's going to take this hard."

"I know. You want me to tell her?" asked Malloy as he reloaded his revolver. He holstered the handgun then checked the breech on the rifle.

"No, I'll do it."

"Well, let's see what's waiting for us," said Malloy.

Cautiously the men approached the cave entrance. Malloy peered out, careful not to expose himself. A shiver went down his back. There was a gentle decline. A few boulders partially hid the entrance that was barely more than a crooked slash in the mountain. The bare rock of the mountain gave way to tall grass and shrubs, high enough to hide men waiting in ambush. Malloy withdrew into the cave.

"See anything?" whispered Colton anxiously.

"No, but something tells me we got a reception committee out there. We need to smoke them out."

"How do you intend to do that?" asked Colton.

Malloy thought for a moment. He needed a decoy or diversion of some sort. While he was thinking, he failed to notice Colton take out a stick of dynamite from his knapsack.

Colton hated to use the dynamite now; but survival was imperative. Besides, he still had one stick left. "Will this help?" he asked, holding the stick of dynamite.

Malloy turned his head and gasped, "Where in hell did you find that?"

"In the armoury. I guess in all the excitement, I forgot about it," replied Colton innocently.

"Give me that." Malloy snatched the stick. Malloy wondered what else Colton forgot to tell him about. Truth was, Henry was turning into a homicidal maniac. It scared Malloy. Taking out the pouch containing the flint, he struck the stones until a spark lit the fuse. He threw the stick into the air. It landed in the thick forest of shrubs. Malloy stepped back into the shelter of the cave. Suddenly there was a tornado of flame, flying debris and bodies.

"Looks like I was right. When they get up to scatter, shoot," ordered Malloy. But just as Malloy finished talking, a rumble echoed through the cavern. The ground quaked beneath their feet. The walls rumbled like a bear awakening from winter's sleep and dust rained on them.

"Shit! The cave's going to collapse. Get out!" cried Malloy Both men hurled themselves through the opening, hit the ground and rolled clear. The mountain shook and roared like a wounded beast. Boulders came raining down from above, bouncing off ledges and hurtling and crashing further down the mountain. Malloy heard a yell. He looked up to see one of the Na'haa natives get crushed by flying rock. He tapped Henry who was lying beside him on the shoulder, "Time to get the hell outta here. Follow me. Stay low." Malloy got to a crouch and began to run.

Clouds of dust hung in the air like thunderclouds. It provided cover for Malloy and Colton. Panic also followed the brief eruption. Colton saw several natives and a couple of Vikings run away.

The men scurried through the brush towards the forest below. Reaching the trees they halted. Malloy was breathing hard. It'd been a long time since he'd had to run so hard and fast. He breathed deep. Hiding behind a tree he looked out and saw two Vikings running down the hill, their war axes swinging above their heads. Malloy aimed his rifle carefully and fired. One of the Vikings screamed and flew backwards. The other kept coming. Colton fired his Winchester and missed. Malloy took aim again and shot the man in the chest. The Viking twisted, fell and rolled down the slight incline coming to a rest not more than fifteen feet from them.

"If you're gonna shoot a moving target, take the time to aim," advised Malloy.

Colton said nothing, and merely glared at Malloy.

"Come on, we have to find Annette. We'll circle back to the palace."

***

"Your majesty," said Hubert softly. He put his hand on Freydis' shoulder.

The Queen, her eyes swollen red from weeping, turned and looked up at Hubert. Cold calm replaced the grief in her face; her eyes burned with anger. She whispered, "Hubert, get Bjarne and the guards. I want the prisoners captured including the woman. They shall be flayed alive for this."

Freydis turned her head and stared into the open dead eyes of her son. She began to hum softly.

"Yes, Your Majesty." Hubert bowed and retreated from the room. On his way down the stairs he met Mary. "Don't go up there. There has been a terrible tragedy. The young prince has been murdered."

"Oh my God!" gasped Mary. "The Queen..."

"She knows. She is there. Come, help me find some of the guards."

***

Annette dreamed of eyes staring at her, cold, lifeless human eyes. She tried to run away but her legs felt like they were shackled. Everywhere the eyes were upon her. She wanted to scream but when she opened her mouth there was no sound. She tripped and fell. Cold wetness seeped through her clothes and chilled her body to the marrow.

Annette awoke. The eyes of dead faces stared down at her from their place on the stone walls. She was lying on the stone floor. Annette picked herself up. How long had she been unconscious? She searched the room for another exit, but there was none. Annette returned to the door. She put her ear next to it and listened. There were sounds of running booted feet. She heard a guard call to another.

"The Queen needs us! Prince Eric has been murdered!"

"Aye, and the prisoners escaped. A battle rages in the mine. But when they're caught, the Queen will have their way with them."

The footsteps faded. Annette swallowed hard and leaned against the door. Her father, Malloy, Colton, and Wilkinson were fighting for their lives. She had to help them, but how? Of course, a diversion! Annette wasn't sure of how many guards there were, but she knew that if the majority were up at the mine fighting, there were only a few around the palace. And if a battle was going on, then Malloy and the others had rearmed themselves. Annette doubted they could cope with two emergencies.

Annette pulled her knife out, then opened the door and peered out into the passageway. It was empty. She went to the great hall. It was deserted. Even though it was daytime, around the room the torches flickered in their holders. Annette pulled a bench over to the wall and standing on it, took down one of the torches. She began lighting the tapestries and furniture. The fire spread, slowly at first, but the dry wood caught and the fire grew to an inferno. Annette ran down the corridor towards the door, lighting whatever she could along the way.

She pulled open the great wooden door. Sunlight blazed in, temporarily blinding her. Suddenly a shadow crossed her path. She looked up to see a guard called Jon in her path. Jon was a broad, muscular young man similar to many of his comrades. He had a dark complexion, green eyes, brown hair, and wore a thick moustache.

"Ha! And where do you think you're going little one?" His eyes glinted lustily at her. Jon had seen Annette earlier during one of her garden strolls and had wanted her; but he had known that Eric had claimed her. Now Eric was dead and the woman had run into his arms. Jon decided he would have some fun with her before returning her to the Queen. Her violet eyes mesmerized him. Never had he seen such color before. He reached out to grab her.

Annette twisted out of his reach. Her eyes never left him. Jon smiled,

"Come, I won't hurt you. I will satisfy the fire in you."

Oh great! Another sex-starved Viking thought Annette. She felt panic rise within her. She took a deep breath as she sidestepped his groping hands. She swung the knife at him.
Jon jumped back. "No wonder Eric wanted you. You're high-spirited. Well, so am I."

He leaped at her, and grasped her right wrist. He twisted gently, but with a firm grasp. Annette felt her hand loosen. The knife clattered on the ground. She spit in Jon's eye and kicked at his groin. Jon brought a knee up and blocked the kick. He twisted her around so that Annette's back was to his chest. He pinned her arms to her sides and dragged her down the steps and into the bush. Annette struggled uselessly.

He tossed her down on the grass and straddled her. Annette tried to squirm out from under him but Jon applied his weight on her. Annette eyed the short dagger in the scabbard on his belt and decided what had worked for Eric would work for Jon; but Jon saw her glance and tossed his dagger out of her reach. "We'll have none of that." His hands grabbed her shirt. Annette grabbed his wrists and tried to push them away.

"Wait, I give up," said Annette. "Let me do it."

"That's better." Jon released her hands.

"First, kiss me."

Jon grinned and bent towards her. Annette poked him in the eyes. Jon bellowed and covered his eyes. Annette wormed her way loose.

"The devil you are girl!" cried Jon.

Annette started to run. Jon leaped and grabbed her ankle. Annette tripped and fell. She tried to get up. Jon, now standing over her, backhanded her. Annette spun and fell on the ground. She put a hand to her cheek. A tear rolled down her cheek. She glared at Jon.

"Enough playing," he bellowed. He undid his belt. Suddenly the young Viking stiffened and fell forward. Annette screamed. There was a knife in his back. She looked up. Malloy and Henry were standing in the grove of trees.

Relief flooded her. Annette got up and ran to Malloy. She hugged him. "Thank you. Thank both of you," she said looking first at Malloy, then Henry.

Henry's face wore a tight smile. So that's how it was. All his suspicions when he was separated from them flooded his mind. Rage coursed through his body. He took a deep breath and said, "Glad we got here in time."

Shouts came from behind. It was then that Annette noticed the smoke pouring out of the palace. She looked up and saw flames shooting out windows.

"I think we'd better get out of here," urged Malloy, "If we can make the river we'll have the canoe. This'll keep them busy. Besides, it'll take them time to check the mine. Let's go."

***

Queen Freydis tore a piece off her gown and covered the lower part of her face. Her eyes stung from the smoke, and the heat was almost unbearable. The great hall was an inferno as she ran through it. Suddenly fire marred her path. She turned ran towards a window, now revealed from the tapestry. She grabbed a smouldering bench and cried out in agony. She released her grasp. The bench clattered on the floor. She'd burnt her hand. Freydis tore off another piece of gown and lay it over a corner of the bench. She pulled the bench towards the window. Stepping up she clambered through window and jumped to the ground.

Smoke and flame consumed the palace. Flames shot from the palace, igniting some of the surrounding trees, and with the breeze that flowed through the valley, the fire spread.

Freydis rolled clear of the palace and picked herself up. Ignoring the pain, she headed towards the road. Anger burned as hot as the fire behind her. Truly she would flay the woman Annette and Malloy for this treachery and cold-blooded murder.

CHAPTER TWENTY-TWO: RAGNAROK

People from the village raced up the road towards the enflamed palace. Smoke covered the area like a blanket. Men and young boys hauled buckets of water from the river. Queen Freydis, in a singed, smoke stained gown tramped over to them. Dirt was streaked across her brow. She looked more like a vagabond than a monarch.

"My Queen!" cried Green-eyes.

"I am fine. Don't try to save the palace. It is beyond help. Save your families. The fire is spreading even as we speak. Find me some of my guards. The outsiders caused this. We must capture them. They will pay for this," she snapped.

"Obi, my Queen" The native turned to a young man behind him and told him to bring some guards. The young man turned and ran up the road towards the mine.

"No doubt they will try for the river. It's the only quick way to escape," said Green-eyes.

"Then we will go after them. Find their trail."

"But my Queen, you can't..." Green-eyes stopped and saw the rage in the great woman's eyes. "Come," he gestured. Green-eyes signalled others to come forward and lead in the fight against the fire.

Queen Freydis and Green-eyes marched swiftly back to the palace. They heard a groan from the bushes by the side of the road. Peering into the clearing near the trees, they saw Jon. Green-eyes jumped the shrubs and went to the dying man. He pulled the knife from his back, wiped it on the grass, and tucked it through his belt. Looking around the native saw the trampled grass. "This way my Queen. I've found their tracks."

Freydis plunged through the grass. She paused to pull Jon's sword from his sheath. "Let's go."

By the time they reached the edge of the village, several of Freydis' guards had joined them. The group left the village with Green-eyes guiding them towards the river.

***

Using the cover of the forest, Malloy, Annette and Colton travelled a parallel course to the main road. Slowly they made their way toward the cliff wall. Two hours later they began to ascend the forested mountain slope. Malloy called a brief rest. Annette sat down under a spruce tree. Colton sat next to her. He was tired and felt like taking a nap. He shook his head. "I'm going to sleep for a week when we get back."

Malloy grinned. "Don't get too comfortable. We can't stay long. They'll be after us."

Five minutes later Malloy stood up.

"Let's go," said Malloy.

"Right," agreed Colton. Slowly, Colton picked himself up. He helped Annette to her feet.

The trio started hiking again. Occasionally Malloy looked up at the mountain wall for landmarks that he remembered. Time passed. The sun grew lower.

"Where the hell is that opening?" wondered Malloy.

"You'd better find it great woodsman. We've no supplies. I'm getting cold," snapped Colton.

"You think you can do any better?" retorted Malloy.

"He's doing the best he can Henry. Be patient." Annette said, "You know, I'm surprised they haven't caught up with us yet." The same thought ran through their minds: maybe they were waiting for them. Malloy checked his rifle. Henry levered a shell into the breech of his Winchester.

***

Queen Freydis' group reached the Asgard Gate.

"There are no signs that the outsiders have passed here yet," reported Green-eyes, after studying the ground.

"Good. Then we will set a trap for them." Freydis turned to the six guards who had joined them. "I want four of you to wait on the other side of the gate. If they get by us, you will stop them. We will hide on this side and try to take them by surprise."

The leader of the guards, a dark-haired slim man named Thorvald chose four men. They followed Thorvald through the tunnel. When they'd gone, the Queen said, "We will make a camp here and wait."

The remaining guard a young bearded man named Snorri took off his cape. "Here your Majesty. It will be cold and we cannot light a fire."

"Thank you," nodded the Queen.

They huddled in some bushes near a grouping of spruce trees and waited. Green-eyes kept watch. The young guard Snorri, scared by the thought of battle, was nervous. He paced some distance away.

"Better you sit down. You make too much noise," said Green-eyes.

Freydis sat with her back against the trunk of a spruce tree. She pulled the cape around her. Even her anger could not keep fatigue from overcoming her. Her eyes felt like iron weights. They started closing. Freydis snapped them open. She must stay awake. Her eyelids fluttered closed. She fell asleep.

***

Darkness closed in around them. The moon came out and lit the landscape in eerie silvery light. They had rested again. Malloy found some edible roots and berries. They ate greedily.

"This is ridiculous," grumbled Colton.

"Have you any other suggestion?" asked Annette. She too was scared and running out of patience, but she had faith in Malloy. Her interest in him was more than an infatuation too. Over the past two months she had grown to love him. Telling Henry scared her. His temper seemed more violent these days. She didn't want to hurt him, but she could not honestly see spending the rest of her life with him. And Malloy, did he feel the same about her? Annette was sure he did, though he had never openly said so. And could she love this land as much as he? Could she give up the trappings of civilized society for life in the bush? The beauty of the land had taken her; but was it enough to sustain her? Her mind was filled with unknown answers. She smiled to herself. Annette, the only worry you have right now is getting out alive. The rest will take care of itself later.

"We could climb over the mountain," said Henry.

"Right, and how are we going to get down? That trail that led up to the opening deteriorated further up. We've not enough rope for climbing down, and you're no experienced climber," said Malloy.

"Better than you old man," snapped Henry.

"Oh really?" Malloy stopped and turned to face Colton.

"Yeah, and when we get out of here, you and I have something else to settle."

"And what's that?"

"Her," snarled Henry, thumbing towards Annette. "I know you've been making goo-goo eyes at her and I don't like. She's mine."

"Have you asked her lately?"

Oh God! Not now. Annette shook her head in disbelief. Here they were out in the wilderness with a troop of wild Vikings ready to kill them and they were arguing about her. It was absolutely ridiculous.

"Well, darling? Are you really interested in this fossil? Hell, he's old enough to be your grandfather." Henry glared at her.

Annette gasped. She was on the spot. How could she? And suddenly she snapped. All the anger, frustration, fear and pain came out. Annette yelled, "This is asinine! We've got more things to worry about than this. Queen Freydis is probably waiting for us with a hoard of her cutthroat barbarians. I know. I saw their chapel with heads hung on spikes. And you two are arguing over me?"

"He started it," said Malloy.

"Listen to you two. Stop acting like children." Annette turned to Henry.

"I'm very--fond of Mr. Malloy, Henry. And quite frankly, you've been a real obnoxious, immature--pain-in-the ass! Now let's stop the bickering right now and get the hell out of here!"

Henry stared at Annette with an open-mouth. He couldn't believe the foulness he'd heard her utter. But it confirmed his feelings. She loved Malloy. They'd probably fucked each other too. She was just like his mother, always ordering, nothing ever good enough. Well, he'd fix the both of them. But Annette was right. They had to get out and Queen Freydis was probably standing by with the troops.

"This way boys and girls," said Malloy. He found a deer path and walked down it. He couldn't believe his own behavior, almost being goaded into a fight by a loudmouthed, spoiled, overgrown child. He'd been trained in the force to deal with situations like this. And everything had been pushed from his mind. He wanted to show-off, and at his age. He was happy though that Annette hadn't told Henry about their shared intimacies. Henry was totally unpredictable, and Malloy didn't want to jeopardize Annette's safety. And yet he wondered if they survived this, would she stay with him? He needed her. Through her he had recaptured his youth, his energy, his life. Age really wasn't much of a barrier. Malloy knew that now. It was your outlook on life that was important. If you were young at heart and healthy there was nothing stopping you. Over the past two months his health had improved. His need for liquor was gone. Malloy craved for life again. For the first time in years he felt almost invincible.

Then, Malloy spotted the crevice. There was a worn trail leading to it through a small clearing. He signalled Annette and Henry to stop. The forest and trees were dense here, providing excellent cover for anyone planning an ambush. They huddled together.

"You two stay here. I'm going to reconnoitre. There's probably a reception committee around, and I'd rather take them quietly by surprise. We don't have enough fire power if they attacked us at once, and we certainly can't risk being taken captive again," whispered Malloy. He shrugged out of the backpack and gave it to Colton. He handed his rifle to Annette, along with a box of extra shells. "You know how to use it?"

Annette nodded.

"What kind of signal will you give us?" asked Colton.

"I'll return. If you start to hear a lot of gunfire make for the opening and run like hell."

"Right."

"Good luck Malloy," said Annette, then she bent forward and kissed Malloy's cheek.

Malloy smiled and nodded, then quietly disappeared into the bush.

An owl hooted. Colton looked up to see some mountain goats silhouetted against the cliff. Silence enveloped them. Minutes dragged like slow summer days. Annette sat against a tree trunk; the rifle propped up between her legs. Fear kept her alert. Her eyes moved constantly.

Malloy snaked on his belly, pausing to listen for any human sound. He had crossed the path and was heading for the crevice when he heard a soft yawn. He froze. Slowly he raised his torso. He saw a figure wrapped in a cape sleeping beneath a tree. Malloy lowered himself and crawled into some shrubbery. Peering out he watched the prone figure, and then glanced around to see if any others were in sight. He watched as a soldier came into view. The Viking stretched and stared down at the lying figure, then turned and walked back into the shelter of the other trees. Malloy crouched and crept forward and around, planning to take the soldier by surprise.

Thorvald paced around the campsite. He was nervous and afraid. He'd never fought in battle before. Though Bjarne and Helmut had trained him, the idea of actually killing someone or being killed didn't increase his courage. Thorvald heard a twig snap. As he started to turn, an arm came around his neck and choked him. A hand as strong as an iron manacle clamped around his right hand and Thorvald felt himself being pulled down. He tried to struggle, but was no match for his opponent. Thorvald gasped for breath. His eyesight became fuzzy. Blackness overcame him.

Malloy pulled the unconscious guard into some bushes and using the man's belts, securely bound him. He cut off the sleeve of the man's shirt and used it for a gag. Malloy put the sheathed short-knife on his belt and took the broadsword out of its scabbard. It was too heavy to carry with him, and Malloy was far from a fencing expert. Instead he hid the sword in another clump of bushes.

Suddenly he heard a shout. Looking up he saw a man with a bow shooting into the clearing at two running figures. Damn Colton!

Malloy swore. He pulled out his revolver and fired. The bowman turned and Malloy instinctively ducked, even though the arrow was off by a yard.

The figure that'd been sleeping under the tree awoke. Malloy saw it was Freydis. Seeing him, the Queen screamed and drew her sword. She charged him. Malloy rolled under the blow, feeling the air of the blade whizzing over his head. He got his feet under him and sprang away just as the sword hit the ground where he'd stood.

"Stand still and fight like a warrior you treacherous bastard!" shrieked Freydis.

Malloy didn't want to kill her, though with the bloodlust in her eye he'd have no choice.

A shot rang out. Freydis whirled around and saw Green-eyes crumple to the ground. Footsteps pounded towards her.

"Stay back!" warned Malloy.

Annette and Colton halted outside the grove of trees.

"There's the bitch that murdered by son!" screamed Freydis and lifting the sword above her head she swung at Annette.

Henry shoved Annette aside. Annette tumbled into the bushes. Her rifle slipped from her hands and fell on the ground. The blade hurled down and pierced the ground. Having no time or room to fire his rifle, Henry dropped it, leaped forward and grasped Freydis' wrists. But the Viking Queen was a strong woman and freeing a hand, clawed at Henry's face. The nails raked across Colton's cheek. He cried out in pain and released her other hand. Freydis snatched up the broadsword and swung towards Annette. "Die Harpy!"

Annette untangled herself from the bush's clutches and leaped aside. The blade swished down and severed several branches. Annette ran towards Malloy who stood with his pistol drawn, trying to take aim at Freydis. The Queen whirled around and charged, swinging the sword above her head and screaming. Annette stumbled and tripped. Malloy fired at point blank range. A red splotch exploded onto Freydis' chest. He fired again. The red stain grew. Freydis staggered and fell on her face. A pool of blood grew under her.

Malloy helped Annette to her feet. "You okay?"

Annette took a deep breath and nodded. "I am now."

Malloy picked up his Enfield. "Come on, there's probably more of them."

They walked over the Colton who stood wiping some blood off his cheek.

"Thanks Henry." Annette squeezed his arm.

"I'll go first," said Henry as they approached the opening in the cliff wall.

It was dark inside the tunnel. Moonlight barely pierced the narrow opening.

"Any torches? Feel along the walls," suggested Malloy. They did. Annette found the holder. Inside was a tightly bound cluster of twigs. "Here it is."

"Bring it over."

Kneeling down, Malloy laid the torch on the ground and took out the pieces of flint. He struck them several times before a couple of sparks fell and took to the wood. Malloy bent close and blew on the embers gently until the fire started. He gave the torch to Colton.

"Lead on MacDuff. I'll keep rear guard."

Colton took the torch and began to walk down the corridor. He smiled. Things were working out better than he planned. They moved walked quietly through the corridor. The passageway grew narrower and Malloy had to turn sideways to make it through. After a short distance the stone corridor widened.

"I think I see moonlight," said Annette.

"Better put the torch out Henry. We don't want to alert anyone who may be waiting outside," said Malloy.

"Okay. But wait here, I'll have a peek first." Henry took the other stick of dynamite out of his knapsack. He lit the fuse, then dashed the torch against the tunnel wall and ran towards the opening.

"Henry! What?" cried Annette.

"Annette!" bellowed Malloy as he reached forward, grabbed her and pulled her back. "Run this way!"

Colton tripped as he ran through the tunnel opening. Suddenly he felt a tornado of air pick him up and hurl him forward. A roar filled his ears and his breath left him as he smashed on the ground. The ground trembled. The mountain shook and roared like a giant beast. Rock and dirt rained down. Colton, his body aching, rolled clear of the tunnel and dashed into the forest. A huge slab of rock slid off the mountain, crashed down and ploughed over two trees next to the one Colton rested against. Dust filled the air and blocked out the moon. Birds screeched and the air was filled with flapping wings. And then there was silence.

The mountain stopped its rumble. The dust cleared and moonlight lit the forest with silvery light. Against the cliff where the tunnel entrance had been was a small hill of stone. A fitting tombstone thought Colton as he stood up.

Colton took a deep breath. His side still ached, but he was alive. And they were dead. Colton smiled. He picked up the Winchester and turned to go. He'd find the canoe and paddle back to the trapper's cabin they'd found. He'd rest awhile then make his way back up the river.

Colton marched down the trail to the bottom of the mountain and stopped. In the small clearing between the mountain and the forest, a wall of human figures blocked his way. They wore helmets and chain mail under their fur vests. Swords, spears and axes were in their hands. One of the figures stepped forward.

"There is a debt to be paid outsider," said Thorvald.

Henry fired his Winchester from the hip. Thorvald staggered back. And then they were upon him.

A scream ripped that night silence, echoed off the mountains and died.

CHAPTER TWENTY-THREE: LIFE AND DEATH

Consciousness seeped back into Malloy. He was aware of a confining weight crushing him. On the other hand, he felt pain and knew that he was alive. He wiggled his legs and arms. They were confined, but nothing was broken. The pain came from rocks that bit into him. His mouth was dry. Dust hovered in the air around him. He felt Annette below him. She coughed and he heard himself mutter, "Thank God."

"Malloy...it's so hard to breathe," she whispered.

"Sorry." Malloy pushed up. "Let me get up, if I can."

A mound of dirt rolled off his back. They were buried in rubble of dirt, rocks and broken timbers. Malloy sat up and twisted. He felt two shoring timbers lying over the dirt that covered his legs. The timbers were wedged against the tunnel walls. It was these fallen beams that saved them from being crushed by the rocks.

Malloy dug his legs free. Annette wriggled out from under him. Luckily they'd managed to clear the main force of the explosion. Freed, Malloy and Annette slowly felt their way to the tunnel entrance. A cool blast of air shot through the tunnel. It revived them.

Dawn was peeking through the darkness when they emerged. A smoky haze blurred the pink and golden sky. Looking up they could see light to the west where the village was. Malloy wondered if the fire was raging out of control. They shivered in the early morning cold. In the pale light they looked like two ghosts. They were covered in dust, their clothing torn. But they were alive. Annette hugged Malloy. He bent over her and kissed her. Annette hugged him. Malloy felt pain in his ribs. The blast must've bruised them.

"Henry tried to kill us," said Annette.

"He was crazy about you. I don't blame him."

"Malloy!"

"It's true, especially the crazy part. Anyway, I'm not worried about him for now. We'll find him, if they don't first."

"Where do we go?" asked Annette.

"Away from here. It's not safe to stay here." Malloy noticed that the bodies of Queen Freydis and Green-eyes were gone. Perhaps the flames were from some sort of funeral pyre. "We've got to get to the river. We'll see if we can find a trail leading over or around the mountains."

Malloy took her hand and they headed off towards the southeast. They hiked at a fast pace despite their fatigue. They'd lost Malloy's rifle in the cave-in and Colton had taken the pack with the few supplies it contained. The last thing Malloy wanted was a battle with the warring Vikings.

***

Colton was barely conscious through the haze of pain that bombarded his senses. After being captured and severely beaten, the Vikings, using barely visible goat trails, climbed and marched back to the other side of the mountain. Henry was carried, bound and suspended from a wooden limb, released partially only when necessary. There were few stops and Henry was given no courtesy as a prisoner. In fact, barely a word had been spoken to him. His ribs ached and he was sure at least two of them were broken. His face was a bruised and swollen mess with one eye swelled shut and his nose broken. Obviously only the orders to bring him back alive kept him from being killed.

Asgard was in flames when they returned. The fire had spread quickly from the palace. The remaining villagers had failed in their attempts to control the conflagration. The people salvaged what they could and set up a tent camp by the lake.

When Thorvald and his small troop marched in carrying Henry the villagers crowded around them. The soldiers pushed the villagers back but did not stop anyone from spitting or throwing rocks at Henry. Several stones hit his legs and arms. Thorvald shouted an order and the soldiers dropped him in the center of the camp. Lying there, Henry raised his head to see a wooden platform in front of him. On it laid the bodies of Queen Freydis and Eric. Wood had been gathered and heaped underneath the pallet. Snorri stood guard over the corpses.

"You captured only one of them?" asked Bjarne.

"The woman and the man called Malloy died in a cave-in caused by this one," replied Thorvald.

"A traitor and murder even of his own kind," said Bjarne as he hobbled forward from the crowd. "Set up a rack," ordered Bjarne to several of the soldiers. He turned to Snorri, "I give you the honor."

"I do not deserve it. I failed in my mission to protect the Queen."

"Then you will redeem yourself," said Hubert. The crowd quieted and parted as the old servant, tall and erect, came forward. There was an aura of command about him. "Sharpen your axe." He stared at Colton.

Turning to Bjarne and Thorvald he said, "See that he is prepared."

Thorvald shouted to the crowd and several men came forward. Colton was cut free and grabbed. A man came forward, his hair was singed, his clothing scorched; he smelled of smoke. Using a knife he slashed Colton's clothing off.

Naked Colton was tied and suspended from a wooden bar propped up by two stout beams in a X formation. His toes barely reached the ground. The men lined up and each took his turn with a leather cat-o-nine tails. Colton screamed as the leather throngs first hit his back. The pain grew until he was swept into unconsciousness.

Night came and the chill of evening woke Henry David Colton. His arms were numb. He shivered and the pain wracked his body. He opened his eyes. At the edge of the camp the funeral pyres were mere embers. Queen Freydis and Prince Eric had been sent to Valhalla. His eyes drifted down his body. His skin was red raw and scored with welts and dried blood.

"You are awake."

Colton's eyes glanced to his right. Hubert stood in the moonlight.

"Your misery will end shortly. In a way, I am grateful to your pompous blundering. The killing of Queen Freydis and Prince Eric was a favor for me, though I regret their loss somewhat." Hubert approached Colton until he stood directly in front of them. "I was the Queen's consort long ago. Eric is my, was my son. He was a foul tempered brut. I guess even my genes couldn't change the centuries of Viking blood. And Freydis could be kind, gentle, and even feminine when she allowed herself to be."

"How," croaked Colton, his curiosity pushing the pain away, "did you come to be here?"

"I was a missionary. I was on my way north to one of the native villages. Unfortunately I was new to the country and didn't realize the hazards of travelling in the autumn. There was a snowstorm. Falling rocks killed my native guide. I blundered about, near death until I was found by several of the Na'haa men who were on a hunting expedition. They brought me here. Freydis was a young Queen back then. She took a liking to me. I was different than anyone she'd met. Naturally I wasn't allowed to leave. When she tired of me, I became her servant. "

"And now?" asked Colton through cracked lips. His voice was low and harsh.

"Thanks to you, I lead these people. Hopefully I shall educate them enough so that they might integrate into the modern world. Their time is long past."

Hubert turned to leave.

"Wait," choked Colton.

Hubert turned back. "What is it?"

"Why? If their deaths were such a favor, why must I die?"

"Justice must still me meted out. It's a crude justice, this revenge, but necessary for these people. I'm sorry. But I can't help you. Even leaders have their limitations. Physically, I'm no match for them; but hopefully mentally I am. Like you, my life lies in their hands." Hubert turned and walked slowly away towards the encampment.

Dawn rose in the eastern sky and Colton was cut down. He lay helpless on the hard earth. His limbs lay useless like leaden lumps of ore. There was no strength left in him. He cursed himself for his self-righteous stupidity. To die like this at the hands of barbarians was an insult to life. And he knew he would never be avenged. Everyone was dead. And he was afraid. Suddenly he craved life, but why he didn't know. Of what use was he like this? Death would be a gift to him; and yet within him arose a primitive instinct for survival.

Two soldiers came forward and picked him up. They half-carried, half-dragged him to a nearby tree stump. One of the men bound his hands behind. His head was placed on the tree stump. Tears rolled down his eyes. He began sobbing uncontrollably. He mustered what little dignity he had left; he took a deep breath and waited.

Slowly they came, men, women and children. They formed a circle around him. The entire village was awake and had come to witness the law being dealt.

Snorri came forward, his axe gleaming in the morning light.

"Don't worry," he told Colton, "you will not endure any more pain. Then you will face your God for what you have done. May you burn eternally in hell."

Snorri raised the blade and brought it down with angered strength. And he'd been right. Colton didn't feel any more pain.

Colton's head was placed on a pike. The pike was rammed into the ground and faced the body now burning at the stake. When the flames consumed Colton's remains, a yell of triumph rippled through the villagers.

Hubert and Bjarne came forward and silence fell over the crowd.

"It is time to leave this place. The Gods no longer favor it. We will go further into the wilderness, away from this civilization," said Hubert. With that the people turned and began packing their camp.

CHAPTER TWENTY-FOUR: HOMEWARD BOUND

It was late morning when Malloy and Annette stopped to rest. They lay down in the shade of a boulder sitting on a mountain meadow. The sun was hot, the air humid. Cumulus clouds rolled across the deep blue sky. Both were exhausted and hungry. Malloy had found some edible berries to snack on; but a more substantial meal was preferred.

"Do you think they're looking for us?" asked Annette.

"No. They'd have caught us by now, I'm sure. They probably think we died in the cave-in. But our troubles aren't over yet."

"I know. No food, no spare clothing or supplies." Annette watched a bird fly overhead.

"But at least I have this." said Malloy, patting his holster. "I'll try some game later. But I want to make sure we're out of hearing range. Just in case."

"I don't blame you. I've had quite enough of Viking hospitality." Annette smiled and shook her head. "I can't believe what we've been through. Why nobody'd believe us." She thought sadly of her father and brother. And it suddenly hit her. She was alone now.

Malloy rolled onto his left side and put an arm over her waist. Annette turned and gazed at him. Malloy felt the violet eyes sear into his soul. She moved closer to him.

"Just hold me," she whispered. And then she cried. Uncontrollably at first, then it subsided into a soft whimpering.

Let it out thought Malloy. All the sorrow, all the pain. Let it flow out and go away. This young innocent woman's been through more in the past two months or so than most people go through in a lifetime. Annette needs love and care and rest. And Malloy realized that it would be up to him to supply it.

He listened to her gentle regular breathing. Annette had fallen asleep. Malloy lay there with her and tried to get his thoughts in order. He had to find a way down the mountain. Once down in the forest they could make their way to Irvine Creek and the canoe. The river would be slow going upstream unless he had a motor. If they were lucky they might run into another trapper or prospector or signal one of the mail planes that normally flew over the area. But that was a long shot Malloy knew. No, it'd be up to them with their perseverance and strength to make it back.

Malloy closed his eyes and let his mind drift. Soon he was asleep.

It was late mid-afternoon when they awoke. Malloy rolled over and looked at Annette. "Feeling better? I think it's time we hit the trail." Malloy stood up and stretched.

Annette blinked and started laughing. "You should see yourself. You look like a ghoulish panhandler."

"Well, you're not a raving beauty either," chuckled Malloy. "We'll clean up at the river." He helped Annette to her feet.

"Which way?" asked Annette.

"Let's keep heading southeast."

Late afternoon Malloy found the goat trail that the Vikings had used. The trail deteriorated partway down. Using whatever handholds and footholds there were, they climbed down. A third of the way from the bottom the trail resumed. And just in time thought Malloy. Their nails were broken, their hands bleeding from tiny rock cuts. Muscles screamed with fatigue from the exertion. Their body was bathed in sweat.

They clambered over a mound of rock and debris that now blocked the tunnel entrance. The rest of the way was easy. At the bottom of the mountain they found Colton's knapsack.

"Look." said Annette as she picked it up. She opened it up. Inside were some matches, rope, and a box of shells, a spare red flannel shirt, and a small leather pouch. She opened the pouch and gasped.

"What is it?" asked Malloy.

Annette passed Malloy the pouch. Malloy peeked in and whistled. Inside, it was filled with gold nuggets. He looked up and smiled at Annette. "Looks like you're rich."

"We're rich," Annette replied, her eyes flashing.

Malloy noticed that some of the grass was still crushed and he saw some dark stains that were probably blood. They'd captured Colton. All the legends flooded his mind, and coupled with the barbaric rituals Malloy had heard about while a prisoner told him that Henry David Colton suffered a fate that no civilized man would've wished on his worst enemy. For the first time since coming home from the war, Malloy prayed. God have mercy on him thought Malloy. He decided not to tell Annette.

As the entered the forest Malloy caught sight of a piece of canvas. He investigated and discovered his pack. One of the straps had been cut.

"Something wrong?" asked Annette, noting the troubled expression on Malloy's face.

Malloy turned and grinned. "No, just thinking. Lots to think about. Come on, we'll get a fire started and I'll see if I can find some real food."

That night they camped in the forest. Malloy shot a squirrel and cooked it over a spit. He made a lean-to and they huddled in its shelter and warmed themselves by the fire.

Sunlight was streaming through the leafy canopy and into their tiny camp when they awoke. They packed up quickly and hiked to the river. There, Malloy found not only the moose hide canoe, but also the good wooden canoe that Green-eyes had used.

They lunched on a trout that Malloy caught and some berries, along with some cold water. Afterwards they bathed. Malloy put on the tan twill pants and blue cotton shirt that had been in his pack and Annette discarded her torn shirt in favor of the red flannel one in the knapsack. Refreshed, they loaded up the canoe and began paddling upstream.

That night they camped under the stars by the river's edge. The broad plain provided little to build a shelter with. Malloy shot a duck. He cleaned it, seasoned it with a few local herbs and roasted it over the fire.

"I don't think I've ever tasted anything so good," said Annette. "You're only saying that because you're starving. When we get back, I'm gonna buy you the biggest steak dinner in Fort Simpson," promised Malloy.

"I intend to hold you to that Duke Malloy."

They ate in silence.

Malloy noticed the clouds rolling in. The air was getting humid. He suspected that it would start to rain either during the night or in the morning. The drops started falling just before dawn. They grew into a downpour. The wind picked up and it made paddling up the river all the more difficult. Waves lapped against the sides of the boat. But Malloy and Annette pushed on. Malloy hoped to make the trapper's cabin by evening.

Time had no meaning. Neither of them had a watch. Clouds blocked the sun. Annette didn't know how long they'd been on the river when she found her strength waning. They'd had no breakfast, and the energy supplied by the previous evening's dinner was gone. The constant rain and wind chilled her and she wished she was listening to the radio and sitting before a fire with a hot cup of tea in her hands.

Eventually Malloy realized the fruitlessness of continuing in the pouring onslaught. They were on the Flat River now and Malloy was still hoping to make the cabin; but fatigue was making the journey difficult enough, without inclement weather. The problem was where to find some shelter. They'd find no dry wood to light a fire and even building a lean-to would be a wet, soggy business. At the same time, Malloy knew they couldn't continue. He could see Annette's strength giving out, and he wasn't even sure how much longer he could keep up. He scanned the shore looking for a place to land. Finally he just headed inland.

They pulled up on a stony beach and pulled the canoe out of the swirling water and into the shelter of a clump of trees sitting like an oasis in a meadow sea. Tipping the canoe over and crawling underneath it, they lay on the wet grass. The rain hit the canoe like a constant drum roll; but Annette and Malloy were beyond caring. They were asleep.

It was late afternoon when they awoke, or so Malloy reckoned by the sun. The clouds had broken and sunshine filtered through. Their shelter had become hot and damp. Not wanting to wait for more rain, they re-entered the river and continued paddling.

At dusk Annette spotted the cabin perched near the rivers edge. Their goal in sight, they paddled furiously with their last ounce of strength. Annette helped Malloy pull the canoe up and ran to the cabin, shouting, "I'll get a fire going and some dinner."

Malloy watched her and smiled. They were going to survive. He hauled out the pack and knapsack and carried them into the cabin. When he entered, Annette was shoving wood into the small potbellied stove. He dropped their supplies and grabbed a tin container of matches off the shelf. He lit the fire.

They stripped and Malloy rung their clothes out, and hung them to dry from pegs on the wall in the cabin. Malloy found a flannel, checkered shirt for Annette and a pair of wool blue serge trousers and a red wool sweater for himself. The sweater was a bit tight, and the pants were ready to fall off him. Malloy used some rope as a belt. They huddled around the fire while Annette opened some tins of corned beef and cooked it along with some flapjacks. Malloy put water on to boil and found a tin of tealeaves. Within minutes dinner was ready and they ate as if it were the first time they had tasted food. Annette made another batch of flapjacks.

"It'll be so good to get back," said Annette, "It feels like I've had one long nightmare."

Malloy nodded as he finished chewing the piece of flapjack in his mouth. "I agree. Nobody'll believe us and it's probably better that we don't publicize what happened."

"I suppose. It can't bring back the dead," choked Annette.

Malloy reached over the table and grasped her hand. "You okay?"

"Yes," Annette whispered. She took a sip of tea. "I'm fine. Thanks."

Afterwards supper Malloy helped Annette clean up. That night they huddled together on the bed that rested against the far wall of the cabin. The heavy Hudson Bay blankets added to their own body heat and the warmth felt good after spending all day in the cold rain. There was a rumble of thunder and lightning flashed, its light giving a blinding eerie light in the dark cabin. Annette rested comfortably in Malloy's arms. Neither of them talked, each caught in their own thoughts. But whatever they might have said kept silent in the wake of an arousing passion caused by their closeness and warmth. Their lovemaking was slow and tender at first. It crested in a frenzy of animal sexuality. Malloy felt Annette fingers grab his skin and her tongue dart in his ear and mouth. He sucked her nipples and his fingers felt the softness of her skin and weaved her hair about them. Outside the storm raged again for a moment, then spent, broke up into night time calm. Afterwards fatigue took over and they both drifted into a deep sleep.

It was the smell of coffee and the sound of sizzling bacon that brought Malloy into consciousness. He rolled over and cracked an eye open. A man was standing by the table mixing eggs in a bowl. Malloy sat up in bed.

The man turned. He was a small-wizened figure with leathery skin and dark bright eyes shaded by heavy lids. He had a prominent nose and a full mouth. Suspenders hitched up his bright red flannel pants. "Morning-why Duke! How yuh doin?"

"Fine. Long time." Malloy sat up in bed, the covers discreetly covering his lower torso. The floor was chilly.

"Glad to see you made yourself at home. Bad storm. Wuz trapping southeast of here."

"Thanks. This cabin was a real blessing. We got caught in it on the river." said Malloy.

"We?" The older trapper turned around. Malloy cocked his head towards Annette's backside. "Oh- I see. Well now." He turned around and Malloy got up and took his clothes off the peg and dressed quickly. He grabbed Annette's clothes and put them on the bed next to her.

The trapper scrambled the eggs and filled two plates with toast, eggs, and bacon. Malloy poured coffee. They left Annette's portion in a pan warming on the stove and went outside to eat.

The coffee scalded Malloy's tongue but he didn't care. It burned through his body reminding him that he was alive. He wolfed down the food, realizing how hungry he was.

"Where you headed now?" asked the trapper.

"Back to Fort Simpson," replied Malloy.

"So am I. Just have to load up my furs. Wasn't a bad season, but the river'll start icin' up soon enough; time to restock my supplies before I go out again. Would you mind the company?"

"Not at all. It's been tough going," replied Malloy.

The old trapper gazed at the river. Malloy's canoe was resting on the bank. "That's some canoe you got. Ain't seen one of them in a long time."

"Yeah, ended up getting it off some Indians. Our boat was wrecked. Wish I had a motor for it though. It's mighty tough paddling upstream," said Malloy.

"Well you just might be in luck. Brought an extra one with me." The trapper got up. "Come here."

Malloy followed the older man to a shed next to the cabin. A three horsepower kicker rested against the wood.

"I'll pay you. I owe you for the supplies we used anyway," said Malloy.

Don't worry about it now. We can settle up when we get back."

"Malloy?" called Annette. She stepped out of the cabin dressed and with a cup of coffee in her hand.

Over here," he called.

Annette followed the voice and saw Malloy talking to another older man. The older man looked toward her as she approached. His eyes brightened and a smile cracked his toothy mouth. He nudged Malloy in the ribs. Annette smiled and came forward, offering a hand. They shook. His hand felt like smooth leather.

"Now I see why you want to get back," laughed the old man.

"Aw, come on."

"He heh," chuckled the trapper, "I'd heard you were taking a party up river. But I didn't.."

"Knock it off." Malloy's face reddened slightly.

"Just jokin." The trapper turned to Annette, "Never did have much of a sense of humor."

Annette grinned back.

"Wuz it just you two?" asked the trapper.

"No, there was another man, he didn't make it back," said Malloy.

"Too bad. It's a beauty of a land, but she's harsh too." The trapper turned and went back in the cabin. "Well, I best start packin'."

"You eat?" asked Malloy.

"Yes. I was famished. Everything tasted so good."

Malloy gazed at her. The sunlight gave Annette's hair a redder tinge. Deep violet eyes shone cheerfully in her tanned, smiling face. She looked radiant thought Malloy. "We'll have company going back, and a motor for the canoe."

"That's very nice, but how will we pay for this?"

"The gold. I'm going to have it assessed when we get back to Fort Simpson. We'll pay him out of that."

"How much do you think is there?" asked Annette curiously.

"Given the current value, I'd say several hundred dollars at least."

They fell silent. Annette put her arms around Malloy and hugged him.

"It'll be so good to get back. I've had my share of adventure for a long time." She looked up at him. "I love you Duke Malloy."

He bent over and they kissed. "I love you too Annie." Malloy looked up. "I never thought I'd say that. I've been shut away from people for so long."

"Your exile has ended." Annette hugged him.

CHAPTER TWENTY-FIVE: FAREWELL FORT SIMPSON

Fort Simpson, N.W.T.
September 15, 1937

It was early morning and the streets were silent in the small northwest town that spread on the shore at the mouth of the Simpson River. The town had expanded with a tent village from many of the Indian hunters who were in getting supplies. Gussy Johanssen was sweeping the boardwalk in front of the restaurant when a booming voice behind him called out, "How about rustlin' up some steak and eggs for a couple of starving prospectors."

Gussy turned and dropped his jaw. The broom fell out of his hands. "Well I'll be hogswallered, if it ain't Duke Malloy and why looky at the lady, a regular woodsman." He chuckled and ran over to greet them, pumping Malloy's hand and put his arm around Annette, steering her towards the door. "Why folks had given you up for dead. Rose got married to some nice Indian lad. So, you find the lost valley of gold Malloy? You rich now? Gonna pay cash instead of credit?"

"Gussy, shut up. No I ain't rich, but I think I can afford your outrageous prices."

"Outrageous?" Gussy halted and shut the door to the restaurant. "Why you knows I'm a fair businessman. Cost money to ship supplies up river. Why..."

"Gussy," interrupted Malloy, "the young lady's starving while you're jawing. We want steak, eggs, flapjacks, toast, and lots of coffee."

"Huh? Oh, sorry Miss, I wuz forgettin' my manners." Gussy opened the door and ushered them inside. "Come on in, and I'll rustle up the best breakfast you ever feasted on."

The smell of coffee made Annette's stomach growl. It'd been a long journey. The river valley was painted in rich hues of orange, red and gold colors. Flocks of geese and ducks were winging southward. Annette saw deer herds on the grassland. The mornings had a cool crispness to them. They were invigorating and refreshing after the hot days of summer. Winter was coming and nature was preparing herself.

"Just as I promised," announced Gussy as he brought two large plates heaped with eggs, bacon, flapjacks, and toast. "The steaks are comin'."

Annette stared at the plate before her. Malloy hadn't said a word. His fork and knife were working overtime. Annette smiled and picked up her fork, wondering how she was going to eat all of it. She almost protested when Gussy returned with two more plates each with a huge deer steak.

Gussy poured them more coffee, then poured a cup for himself and pulled up a chair. "Now tell me all about it. Say, whatever happened to that young feller that wuz with you. Can't remember his name, but he was a pompous ass."

Malloy paused, "We got separated. Found some of our supplies, but no sign of him. I suspect he's dead."

"Oh," said Gussy, "That's too bad." He looked up at Annette. "Sorry missy."

"Thank you," said Annette quietly.

"You sure look in good shape Malloy," complimented Gussy, "Don't he?" He tapped Annette on the shoulder.

Annette put her fork down. "Yes he does."

"And you, why the fresh air and sunshine done wonders for you. Why if I wuz forty years younger, I'd..."

The door opened and a couple of local trappers came in. "How about some grub Gussy. We're starvin'."

"Okay, okay." Gussy waved a hand at them. "Well, best get at it. Enjoy the meal. Talk to you later."

"Peace at last," mumbled Malloy.

"Aw, he was just being nice. It's good to be back with people," said Annette.

"I suppose." Malloy smiled. "Gussy's quite a character."

"Yes he is," agreed Annette. "Oh, I don't know how I'm going to eat all this."

Malloy glanced at Annette's plate, now three-quarters empty. "I'd say you were doing a good job of it."

"Really Malloy."

Malloy put down his coffee cup. "I'll be back to settle with Gussy. I have to see Claude Marchand and go over to the Assay Office."

Annette nodded.

"After you finish, get a room at the hotel. I'll meet you there." He stood up.

"Malloy."

Malloy looked around. Gussy was busy in the kitchen and the other men were reading a two-week old newspaper while waiting for their meal. He bent over and kissed Annette on the cheek. She smiled at him. Malloy nodded and left.

Annette took a sip of coffee and chuckled over Malloy's embarrassment about showing affection in public.

Constable Claude Marchand groaned and wished the pounding would stop. Why had he drunk so much that night? But he knew the answer: Fort Laird. How the hell was one to keep his sanity living in this godforsaken region? He rolled over and put the pillow over his head. But the pounding continued. And this time he heard a voice.

"Claude! Haul your ass out!"

Claude tossed the pillow aside and blinked. Daylight streamed through the window over the bed. He pushed himself up. The pounding was coming from the door. "ALL RIGHT. I COMIN'!" His head pounding like a bass drum Claude stood up and climbed into his blue serge trousers with the yellow strip down the side. In stocking feet he wandered out of the bedroom and through the office area to the door. He moved the shade aside. "Sacre blue!"

He unlatched the lock and opened the door. "Malloy! You're alive! We tawt dat we may have to go lookin' for you."

"Nice to see I'm welcome." Malloy strode into the office and sat down in the wooden armchair by the desk. "Your emotional tribute is overwhelming."

"Aw shut up." Marchand marched past Malloy and sat down at the desk. He pulled out a bottle and two dirty glasses. Malloy waited until the drinks were poured.

"Salute!"

They touched glasses and swallowed the shot. It burned all the way down. Malloy shook his head. "Holy shit!" He made a face and put the glass down.

"Bin a long time, eh?" Marchand chuckled. "Well, at least dat hangover, she gone."

"I have a report to make."

"Really. Someone died, I take it?" Marchand propped his feet on the desk and leaned back in the armchair. "By du way. I got dat report on Colton." Marchand grinned like a junkyard dog that just caught an intruder. "His father was named Wilkinson. How you like dat? Coincidence,eh? Boy worth plenty."

"Not dead he's not," replied Malloy, "And no, I didn't kill him. Though he deserved it. He tried to murder Annette Bouchard and myself."

"You play wit fire, you get burnt." Marchand wagged a finger at Malloy.

"Sounds like you got de motive."

"I didn't kill him. Fact is he was a greenhorn. He thought he knew better than everyone else."

"So what happened out dere?" pressed Marchand.

"As far as I know he got eaten by grizzlies." Malloy looked Marchand straight in the eyes.

"Ou 'ave to do better den dat." Marchand swung his legs down and sat up in the chair. He opened a drawer and pulled a form out, then fished around in the middle desk drawer for a pencil.

"You won't believe me," warned Malloy.

"I bin stuck in dis hell place for trois years. I seen or heard everyting. What happened?"

And Malloy told him. A half an hour later, Marchand looked down at his notes. He shook his head and tore up the report. He looked up at Malloy. "He got lost in de woods and a grizzly she eat him."

"I told you."

"Ah." Marchand waved a hand at him. "And dere waz all dat gold you say?"

"Yeah, a whole mountain full; but you can't spend it if you're dead. The owners took rather an exception to that. Besides, we didn't return entirely empty handed. It'll give Annette a new start."

"And you. She's a pretty one Duke. You not let her go. You got noting here. Rose, she plenty mad at you. Married nice Indian boy down river. Next year she be fat and pregnant."

"No doubt you're right." Malloy let his eyes wander around the sparse office. Now that he was back, the land pulled at him once more. And while the beauty of the country was engraved in his mind, he knew he would miss it. It had been a long time since he'd lived in a city. He wasn't even quite sure what he would do. The money from the gold certainly wouldn't last forever; and yet there was Annette. The way she had talked, he knew that she couldn't be happy living the simple life of a trapper and prospectors wife. She proved she could go the distance, but her desires were more the trappings of civilization. And as for himself, he knew that he needed her. Sacrifices were always required in relationships, and in this one it was required.

"Malloy, are you all right?" asked Marchand.

Malloy shook out of his reverie. He grinned at the Mountie.

"Yeah, I'm just fine." He stood up and offered a hand to Claude.

"Thanks."

They shook. "Don't mention it. For I certainly won't mon amie."

Malloy walked to his cabin. The sun was up. Its warm light trickled through the trees that overhung the trampled dirt path. A cool breeze rustled the branches. Birds chirped and insects buzzed. The

forest was alive. He saw a squirrel zip across the path. And there in a
clearing by the river was the cabin. As he approached it, Malloy
realized that it no longer felt like home. Malloy took the key that hung
behind one of the doorframe beams. He unlocked the door and entered.
The cabin was cool and musty. Rose had cleaned up. The bed was
made, a wilted flower sat in a dried out glass vase on the table. The
dishes were stacked neatly on a shelf over the sink. Malloy opened the
footlocker that sat at the end of his bed and opened it. He pulled out
the remnants of his old army uniform and threw it in a corner. He went
to the wooden bureau and emptied the contents, drawer by drawer into
the footlocker. He took off his holster and packed it with his clothes.
He took his few books and laid them on top. He looked around, but
there was nothing else he'd need. He hefted the locker on his shoulder
and walked out. Malloy didn't even bother to lock the door.

Annette lay naked on the cool, soft bed. She'd finished her
breakfast and had taken a room, ordering a bath. After bathing in the
hot springs, the metal tub seemed cramped; but being clean and
refreshed brought its own rewards.

There was a knock at the door. Annette grabbed her robe and
slid into it. She tied the cord. "Who is it?"

"Malloy, who else?"

Annette opened the door a crack. Malloy stood in the hall
with a metal footlocker hefted onto his right shoulder.

"Well?"

Annette smiled and opened the door. Malloy entered and
dropped the footlocker by the end of the bed. The floor shook and
some water from the tub sloshed up and spilled.

"Shall I order some clean water?" asked Annette.

"I suppose I do need one." Malloy began to unbutton his shirt.
"By God I've bathed more in the past couple of weeks than I
have for years."

"I wouldn't brag about it."

"You're a saucy one." Malloy grinned. He tossed the shirt on
the bed, kicked off his boots, and began to unbutton his pants. Annette
sat on the bed and watched him. "I went to the Assay Office. Old
Jake's eyes nearly fell out of his head. It'll take him awhile but he said
he'd let me know before suppertime."

Malloy stepped out of his pants and began to unbutton his long
johns. He became acutely aware of Annette's gaze. "Haven't you got
something to do?"

"After all we've been through, you feel shy Duke?" Giggled Annette. She loosened her tie and the robe fell open. She leaned back on the bed.

"Damn you, you liberated female," muttered Malloy.
He dropped on the bed next to her.

"The water'll get cold," said Annette. Her hands pushed his hairy chest away.

"It already is." Malloy grabbed her and kissed her.

Old Jake turned and lifted his baldhead towards the sound of the open door. The Assay office was empty. Jake had been running some tests on a sample brought in by one of the local prospectors. A wide grin broke out across his face when he saw Malloy and Annette. Malloy looked tan and fit; the woman was a dandy in her tweed dress and light brown blouse.

"Where'd you find this ore?" he asked.

"Why?" replied Malloy.

"It's one of the richest I ever seen." He wiped his brow with his handkerchief. "And I can't buy it all off you. You'll have to go into a big city to cash this in." Jake handed the pouch to Malloy.

"Is there enough for travel money to Yellowknife?" asked Malloy.

"I expect so." Jake opened up a metal box and handed Malloy a wad of bills. "And The Distributor's due day after next. That'll take you to Hay River, unless of course you want to hitch a ride on the mail and supply plane. There's a regular flight leaving tomorrow. Go see the fellows over at United Air Transport. She comes in tomorrow."

"Good." As Malloy started to count it, Annette took the pouch from him and put it in her purse.

"Say, where'd you find this vein?" Asked Jake.

"That's all there is. The place where it was is buried." Malloy had five hundred dollars. He looked up at Jake. "And I think it'd be wise if this were kept quiet."

"I know. People are pretty good around here; but gold does strange things." Jake winked at Malloy.

They left late the next morning. Malloy had booked them passage on a United Air Transport flight. The plane was a six passenger Bellanca. Annette settled into her seat and took a magazine from her purse. It was a two-month old copy of Life that Malloy had gotten from Claude Marchand. She glanced over at Malloy. He looked uncomfortable in the cramped seat, and nervous. Though he hadn't said anything, Annette suspected that if this wasn't his first flight, it'd been a long time since he'd flown. She squeezed his hand reassuringly. Malloy turned and grinned at her, then looked back out the window.

As the plane rose over the small settlement, a lump settled in Malloy's throat. He looked out at the expanding wilderness below with its dense forest and majestic mountains. And knew that he'd never be back.

EPILOGUE

December 24, 1940
Montreal, Quebec

The storms of war dispelled some of the glitter and joy that was normally felt during the season. The country and the city were converting to a bunker mentality with the news of the Nazis sweeping Europe. In the garment district uniforms were being turned out instead of business suits. At industrial sites around the city, chemical plants were at work inventing news ways of death. Tanks, cannons and rifles were taking the place of cars and trucks. Aircraft that dropped death instead of delivering passengers were being churned out as fast as possible. For those not fighting on the front, there were jobs and an opportunity to profit from man's destructive nature. It was a relief from the ' dirty thirties'.

    A dark gloom hung over the old city. Snow fell like propaganda leaflets. The wind swept it along and deposited it unevenly on the streets and sidewalks. It was after seven and he was late. Duncan Malloy, a little grayer, pulled the collar of his topcoat closed as he strode down the street towards the trolley stop. Annette had needed the car in order to go to a Doctor's appointment. With the weather turning worse, Malloy had called her and told her he'd take a cab or a trolley. Being without a car wasn't a problem. Most of his clients were in close proximity. But Annette would be worried and a little angry. She was four months pregnant and already Malloy noticed the changes in her personality that he'd heard about from other husbands who'd suffered under their wives with the same condition.

    The past three years had been difficult, but good for them. Malloy had cashed in the gold nuggets for almost one thousand dollars. They'd used the money to rent an apartment, purchase some necessary furniture, and clothes. The balance had supported them while Malloy and Annette both looked for work. Annette found a job as a secretary with a law firm; for Malloy it'd been tougher, especially given his age. With his experience as a trapper he landed a job as a buyer of furs for a wholesale company in the city. That had necessitated a fair amount of consistent travel; something that Annette wasn't overly pleased about. Later though while working late, Malloy had thwarted some thieves attempting to make off with a quantity of furs. The man he worked for, a Mr. Herman Koss, then learned about Malloy's military and police experience. Malloy then became chief of security.

    Over the past two years Malloy investigated and discovered a number of companies in the business that required security. Realizing a need, and spurred by the thought of once again being his own boss, he managed to gain several contracts. He hired a few good men, most were ex-policemen like himself, and set up a small security business, dealing exclusively with furriers. Now, two years later with the war and the threat of sabotage, Malloy expanded and managed several contracts with some armament and chemical companies who were subcontracted by the military establishment. With his modest business firmly established, Malloy and Annette were planning on purchasing a house of their own. Tonight he'd been doing rounds checking to make sure all his men were on duty. Malloy was tired and hungry. As he rounded the corner a lanky huddled figure ran into him.

"Excuse me," said the figure, as he straightened his hat.

"S'all right. No harm done." replied Malloy. And in that instant he saw the look of surprise and horror revealed by the streetlamp of the fellow pedestrian.

"Say.." began Malloy. But the words were barely out of mouth when the man hurried across the street and disappeared into the mists of the falling snow.

Malloy reached the trolley stop and waited. He checked his watch. The streetcar should be along in the next few minutes, or he might be able to flag down a cab. Malloy looked back down the street and shook his head. The figure had disappeared into the night. He had recognized the man, just as he'd been recognized. After all, it'd only been three years. And that's why he didn't spend time puzzling about why Freydis' old servant Hubert was walking the streets of Montreal.

THE END

Printed in the United States
94525LV00001B/7-30/A

9 781894 936811